The Missing

Seven Stories

Tory Tuttle

Contingency Street Press

Copyright © 2023 by Tory Tuttle
All rights reserved.
No portion of this book may be reproduced in any form without written permission from the publisher or author, except as permitted by U.S. copyright law.
All characters appearing in this work are fictitious. Any resemblance to real persons, living or dead, is purely coincidental.
Library of Congree Control Number: 2023904153
ISBN: 978-1-958015-02-5 (pb)
ISBN; 978-1-958015-03-2 (eb)
Logo art: Janet Glovinsky
Cover design: Suzanne Hudson

Contents

Dedication	IV
1. I Saw Him Sleeping	1
2. Horizontal Hold	30
3. 112 Months	45
4. Next Stop	74
5. Stranger	92
6. The Bridge	107
7. Stray Socks	118
About Author	132

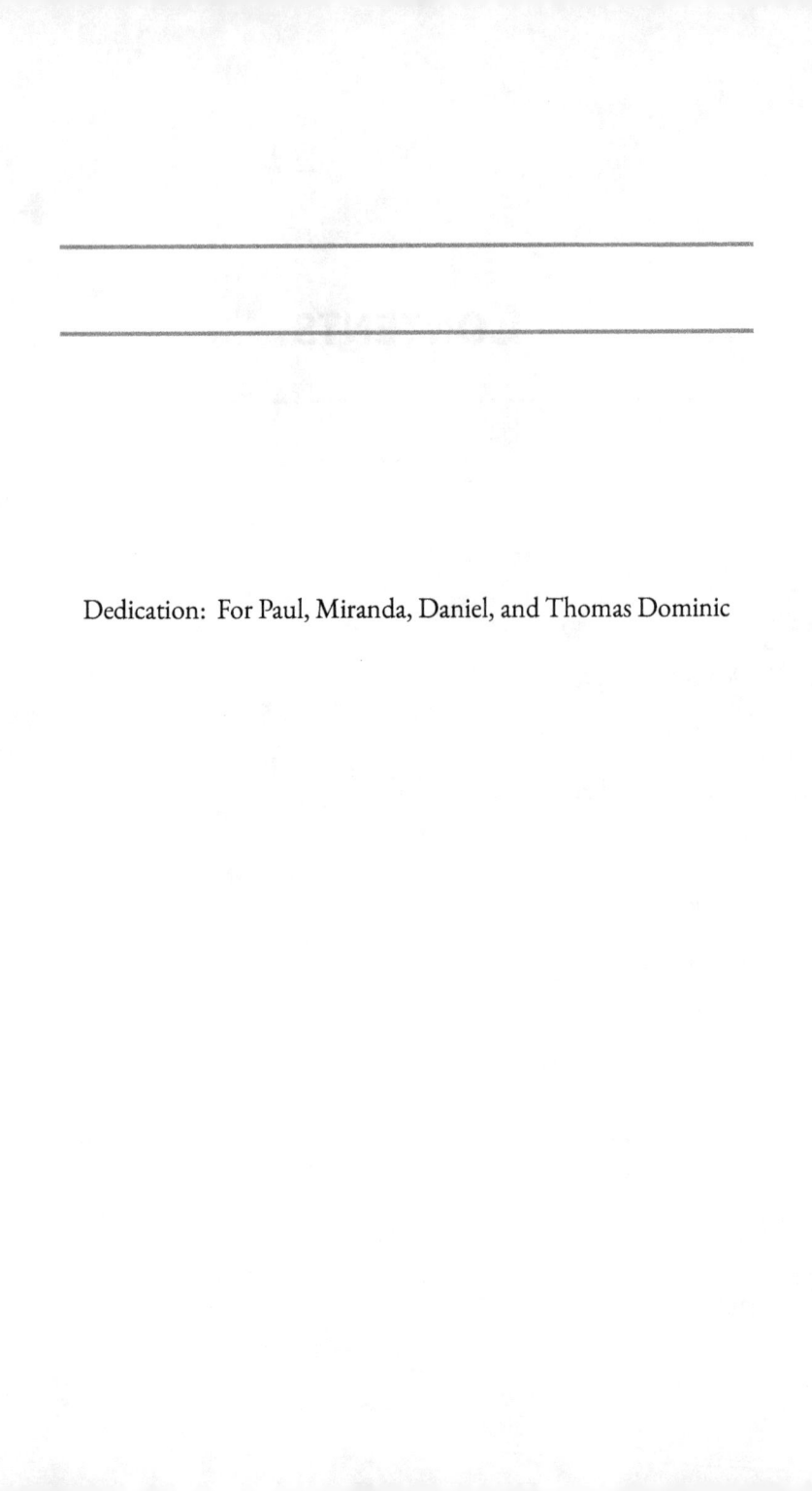

Dedication: For Paul, Miranda, Daniel, and Thomas Dominic

I Saw Him Sleeping

We took the D bus to Denver, Carlos and I did, and then we waited at Market Street, waited and waited till the bus to Salt Lake arrived, sometime before midnight. We were sitting on a bench and his head drooped toward me, then straightened up, as if he was determined not to fall asleep. Did it matter? Was he keeping guard for me? Was he scared I'd see him asleep and helpless? There were, standing around us, transfers from the Omaha bus, waiting, sleeping on their feet, stumbling like statues on the move. Carlos knew, didn't he, that I'd seen him asleep at his sister's, once or maybe twice. Maybe he didn't know, since he was asleep, those afternoons. At the bus station, the homeless had settled on the benches farthest from the bus lanes. Small mountains of men trying to pretend they were sitting, not lying, on the benches. They were men, I was thinking, but you couldn't tell, could you, whether the bundles were men or women, whether the blankets were black or gray. When we first sat on the bench, waiting, Carlos put his arm—like a blanket—around me. I was huddled, was I homeless? When you're on the run, you don't know. Don't think about it—not about your brother, not about your mom. Think about hiding, about not getting caught. Or don't think—just move.

The first time I saw him sleeping under the window, we were at his sister's, and I thought of Manuel. That time, the first time, Carlos lay on his stomach, his mouth slightly open, maybe he was drooling, and his lashes looked longer than they really were. Manuel's lashes are quite as long as they seem. When you think about it, Carlos, asleep, was not much like Manuel. He was probably younger than Manuel, maybe fifteen, and not as pretty. Sunlight on the pillow touched the end of Carlos's nose.

I don't want to think of Manuel. Not now, not anymore.

Carlos had said we were going to his cousin's place outside Salt Lake, but we weren't there yet. We were just sitting on a bench, and all the same we were on the run. Those cousins—did they know we were coming, did they even know? I wouldn't ask, not me. It's not as if I knew Carlos all that well. It had been a month, maybe less, since the first time he followed me. Carlos had been hiding behind a thick tree I passed on my way back to the Residential Treatment Center. They let me walk the fourteen blocks from the high school. "Hey, Marcella," Carlos had called the first time, "I've been waiting for you, you know." I couldn't let him come to the RTC, and I was just as glad. I was fourteen, almost fifteen, and it had been a while since I could go to my home, to my mom's. It wasn't very long before I was visiting him at his sister's. Not long before I watched him asleep.

The first time was late one afternoon at his sister's. His sister's name was Lola, is Lola, and she has a small apartment in north Hamilton. Scrunched up beside Carlos, I closed my eyes, but the cars going by on High Street kept me awake, the rush of one car after another, the car's sound gathering and releasing, gathering and releasing. Carlos said the sounds of those cars put him to sleep. He slept in the day because of the men who came to Lola's place in the evening, and in the night. The men stumbled around the apartment, Carlos said, mumbled along with the music, smoking dope, arguing about the price of weed and Cheerios and coke. Carlos didn't smoke, not at all, and he didn't like it when I did. Why should he care? I thought, but I didn't say anything. Most of the time, it's easier to say nothing. Carlos couldn't sleep at night, and in the afternoon I could never sleep, so I watched him for a little while, then I climbed off the couch, stepping around Carlos carefully, awkwardly, so I wouldn't wake him, moving over to the front window where I pulled back the curtain, trying to decide whether to leave or not to leave, and the cars went on by. Trees line High Street, all along High Street, and that afternoon tiny leaves let the light through. This was the season of tiny leaves, pale green, jewel green, grass green. Back at home there would be small leaves on a tree right outside Manuel's window. These High Street leaves danced and rustled when the big bus lumbered on by. One tree had tiny buds that resembled red beads. I left Carlos sleeping and went down into the street on my way back—not to my mom's, but to the RTC where I'd been placed back in March. I looked up at the buds and stretched my hand up toward them, but I couldn't reach. I left the buds and kept walking. I had to be in by 6:00. On the way, I saw more than one tree with the same red buds. The next day, when it snowed, the red buds fell like beads and decorated the snow, and when the snow melted, they lay on the asphalt, dirty-red and flattened by tires.

It wasn't so hot in Utah when Carlos and I got off the bus. I thought it would be, with the desert and all. There was a lot of bright sky, even in the city with all the trees growing around all the houses. We walked and hitchhiked in the cold under the white bright sky to where Carlos's cousin, Alberto, lives outside Salt Lake City. I wanted my coat that was, maybe, still huddled on the end of my bed at the RTC. The RTC was hardly a home, but my bed was my bed, and maybe my coat was waiting there now. We had to hitchhike because even though Carlos had saved money from his Safeway job, that money was gone now. "Shit," Carlos had said at the information window in Denver when they told him the price of the bus tickets. Carlos had his cousin's address on a piece of paper, but it took us a while to find Peach Tree Court. His cousin, Alberto, had babies and a wife, Renata, who wasn't so happy to see Carlos and me arrive, but she didn't complain too much, not out loud. The babies were a little girl and a boy who was littler. Alberto and Renata were afraid another one was on the way. That's the way, you know, wherever I live—babies and more babies on the way. Back when we lived in Denver, there was that girl across the hall I used to kiss—I can't remember her name for sure, Emilia? Theresa? I was pretty young then, in the third or fourth grade, we were in my aunt's apartment, across the hall from Emilia. The boyfriend, Freddy, would come and sing to Emilia (or Theresa) and pull her hair and leave, or he'd hit her cheek so the next day it would be like a peach, and one of her eyes would be an unhappy slit. When he left, she'd cry that she'd never let him in again, but she was pregnant and worried. I'd kiss her cheek or her eye, but I couldn't say, "Don't worry." She was just beginning to show—she still wore her old jeans, but she had to leave the zipper undone. I was never going to let that happen to me. There are ways, lots of ways, to escape that, I thought. I never found out what happened to Emilia or her baby because after two months we moved back to Hamilton. By now, probably, her babies have babies.

That first morning at Alberto's we sat at the kitchen table with him and with Renata, and their babies kept climbing on her lap and climbing off. I felt cold in my fingers and at the back of my neck. Carlos said he was going to get a job, and I was going to get one, too. I could work at the movie theater, or in the kitchen at the hospital. So—we were on the run, but we'd settled in. Should I really be scared? I could let Manuel know, write his friend Fernando like he said, let Fernando know where I was.

Finally, I was living in a place that was not the RTC. It's what I wanted, wasn't it, so shouldn't I be glad, not scared, not cold? And I was with Carlos—didn't I want that? I didn't know—I never seemed to know. When he first followed me at the end of April, he crept along, half-a-block back, then darted ahead and hid behind a tree. It was almost May, then. I'm always so glad when it is finally May, but spring doesn't help much in the long run, not when it snows, and that May it snowed, day after day. My shoes were always wet. Sometimes it rained when it snowed, and grass would show. Sometimes the snow would pile up on the grass, up to four inches or maybe five. The cars going by were even louder than usual on the snowy wet street, even dirtier.

That first time Carlos called out to me, we were just two or three blocks away from the RTC, and I wasn't at all sure I wanted him waiting for me, but he was nice enough then. He'd touch my arm, just a little, look for a long time into my eyes, his mouth just a little bit open. But he couldn't come in. The RTC has plenty of rules about what time you have to get home and who can come in, when you have to clean the bathroom, and when to change your sheets. I didn't need any points against me, not then. I didn't want to go back to detention, that's where I was before. Manuel was still in detention—I thought he was. They sent us there, after they busted into my mom's house and found us in Manuel's room. You have to wonder, each time, how long Manuel will last in detention—he hates it so.

I talked to Carlos under the tree. I watched him watching me, and after just a little while it started to snow. I had to go in, I said. It was almost curfew, I said. I was not about to freeze out in the snow.

That spring the winter weather lasted way too long, the snow and the cold. It makes you old, very quickly, being cold. Very soon, I thought, I'd be as old as the couple that hitchhikes up the canyon in the evening, up to where they lived in Raven City. In the morning they'd come down from Raven and fly their cardboard signs at the exit from the Safeway lot, or on the corner of Shady Gulch and High Street. When they came back up Shady Gulch in the evening, they'd hold hands sometimes, as they walked across Sixth Street with the light. And they were old. Maybe she was pretty once, but she had lines of tiredness and cold all over her face. He had hair flying out in every direction, and he was tall, skinny like an old skeleton ready to crumble. I thought, sooner than you know I'll be old like that, and Carlos won't be one to walk up Shady Gulch with me toward Raven City. At any rate, who'd want to live in Raven? Sooner than you think, my mom will be old like that. Next time I go to see her, I don't want her looking old, not so old.

I always want to see my mom. I'm always missing her; then when I see her, I don't know why I think it matters. What are we thinking? What is there to say? Maybe she'll tell me about Leandra who finally kicked her boyfriend out. Or she'll mention Ramón, how he complained, once again, about that double play in the Panthers' game, about the daffodils fading in the smoky-glass vase. She'll never say he's been skipping school, he's borrowed Uncle Rick's car for more than two days, he hasn't called and he's been gone almost a week. Ramón's her favorite, after all. Ramón's everyone's favorite—mine as well, but I love Manuel the most. She'll tell me about Nora and the baby, who still live with my mom. Most likely Mom won't talk about Manuel who's maybe in detention, who's maybe run again. It's easier to talk about babies and there are always babies—wherever I live—babies and more coming. My oldest sister, Leandra, had little Ricky and Adrianna; they lived with us when I was ten or eleven and my dad would come sometimes then, come shouting and stamping into the living room, and my mom would end up chasing him away with whatever she could grab, a broom, a knife, or even a fork, the one with the bent handle. Every foster home had a baby or more, and Alvaro and Filippa had three babies when I lived with them. At the RTC we'd look around and guess who was pregnant. They gave us birth control pills every morning, but of course the pills didn't always work. At the RTC, after all, they don't manage to keep track of who is where on her cycle.

When I'm on the run, when I'm in detention or at the RTC, I think of all those babies born and waiting to be born. I think of my mom talking, think of my sitting sideways on a chair after a bath as she combs out my hair, as she reaches out to push a baby in his swing. Not that she ever combs out my hair anymore. Her own hair she does comb out carefully and makes it look very nice.

At Alberto and Renata's, I didn't write Manuel's friend—not for a long time—and I didn't find a job, not for a while. Maybe Carlos had a job—he was gone a lot, mostly at night; he had money, once in a while. Once in a while, I watched the babies when Renata went out. Usually, I'd leave in the morning before or soon after Alberto and Renata got up. At first, when I was supposed to look for a job, I wandered around the shopping area close to Peach Tree Court. I saw the movie theater, but I didn't know where the hospital was. I was scared they'd ask how old I was if I walked into the theater or the hospital, they'd ask to see ID. I was fifteen, almost, but even with a lot of makeup, I didn't look older than that, maybe I looked younger, and I didn't have an ID, not one I could show them. Also, I didn't have to smell the popcorn in the theater to know it would make me feel sick. In the afternoon or evening I'd go back to the little house and sit on the corner of the couch, pretending no one saw me there. I'd go for a walk and another walk. I didn't want to come back unless Carlos was there; I didn't want him to be there. I was feeling a little tired, a little strange. All that walking, after all, is bound to make you tired.

At night we slept in the living room, on the single mattress kept behind the couch: we'd push the couch into the center of the room and lay the mattress flat. I didn't tell Carlos how I felt, but I thought maybe he knew. He wasn't on me as much. During the day we stood the mattress on its side against the wall and pushed the couch back against it. I kept my backpack, flattened, under the couch. You'd never know we were there.

In the early morning, because I woke up way before Carlos, I had time to lie and listen to the birds walking in the gutter, the uneven fall of early morning raindrops. I don't always like that time of day. Sometimes Carlos turned over, his fingers touching me one at a time, and his cute little penis touching my leg. Sometimes I'd fall back to sleep and dream about lively piano music entering the living room, along with a lot of people with sex on their minds. Sometimes, in the dream, you hardly knew who was singing and who was crying, who was on top of you and who was inside you.

I'd get tired of lying there, bored, and I didn't want to be the bored person in bed with someone else, so I'd get up, sit on the couch, and watch the sun come up into the living room window. When I was with Manuel, I never woke up in the morning. When I was with him, in his room, it would be afternoon, once in a while, or early night if no one else was at home. I never slept. I was not bored, but sometimes Manuel would fall asleep after we did it and I would watch him. Now, I wanted to watch him again. I needed to hear from him again. He told me in May to write his friend Fernando, and I finally wrote to Fernando on a postcard—you don't have to put many words on a postcard. I mailed it and immediately counted the days before Manuel would answer. Of course, after five days, after seven, he did not answer. Carlos, each day, slept later and later. He was gone in the afternoon and into the night. Only once in a while would he wake me when he got home, with his fingers not his mouth, not gently; then he'd climb on top. For a small person, he could be heavy. This wasn't making love. It was being quiet as you could be in that small house, not making noise, not at all.

He had money sometimes. Sometimes he did not, and a lot of the time he was mean. It's not that he hit me, but I was afraid a lot, and maybe I was homesick, but for what home? I wanted Manuel—when would he come? I wanted my mom, of course. But even if she was not two hundred or four hundred miles away, I couldn't go see her. Two years ago, or three, I tried to see her when I was on the run. I wanted to see her one time for a little while, for a little while stop being so alone. I went at night and looked in the windows of her apartment. I could see nothing except a decorated comb inside on the window ledge. I ran away, maybe I was crying.

When I was in Hamilton, walking up High Street to Carlos's place, I thought more than once about turning east on Evergreen and walking on out to my mom's. That would be quite a long walk. Later, I wished I had gone, but, you see, I was not allowed to go to my mom's, and, anyways, they might catch me there. She was living in Little San Pedro then, and she had a little house—not an apartment. The house was pale blue with two bedrooms. It was not any bigger than an apartment, with not much of a yard—some dirt in the front, grass in a few clumps, trying hard. Still, it was not a trailer but a house, a manufactured home, standing up by itself alongside the other Little San Pedro houses. I was not allowed to go there: in March, when they released me from detention, they gave me the conditions of my assignment to the RTC. These said where I was not to go—not to the bus station, not to the downtown mall, not to my mom's. These said where I was to go—to the RTC, to Hamilton West High School. In between, they'd let me walk—it's about ten blocks if you go west on Apache and up the hill on Ninth or Sixth or one of the little in-between streets. Sometimes, I'd just go back to the RTC from the high school. Sometimes, though, I'd take a long way, sometimes a longer way up to north Hamilton.

Carlos had stopped showing up during my trek back from school. After a little while, I wondered why, and I'd go north on High Street to his sister's apartment. Each time I came back to the RTC, I thought I wouldn't go again to Lola's place. Sometimes Carlos was hard, his face turned hard and flat, like a frying pan that hasn't been washed in a while. You can't tell what he is thinking. You don't always want to know. It would be much better not to go back, not ever again; still, some days you have to see someone outside, and you can't see your mom, you can't see Manuel who used to tease you, who'd sent you a letter, just once. You just have to go: you end up cutting sixth and seventh period to visit Carlos while his sister is at work. When you come in, Carlos says he's just back from work, from Safeway where he's a bagger.

Often enough when I got to the apartment on north High Street, Carlos grabbed me if no one was home. I could tell he was tired and bored and he didn't waste time on kissing, and sometimes just to see what would happen, I'd fight back at him. Carlos could get fierce, as if fierceness mattered. Sometimes I liked it, sometimes I wanted to laugh. It's nothing new to me. Since I was little, there's been plenty of practice, dealing with the fierce and angry ones, practice with my father, my brother, the building supervisor, Nora's baby, my boyfriend, my cousin, my other brother. It's just something people do to keep from being bored, something that happens when you have to hang around people. I didn't know how long I'd have to hang around Carlos— there was no one else, right then, not even my mom. Twice a month I was supposed to see her for supervised visitations. But did she remember to come? Maybe once, I think, maybe two times. I saw her in the little room off the main living room of the RTC. Supervised visitations just meant that Mrs. Garvey or Andrea could stick in their heads any time they felt like it. Most of the time they didn't feel like it—why bother? After all, what could we say that they'd want to listen to? Mom told me Nora's baby gets into the magazines and spreads them all over the rug. Would Mrs. Garvey want to listen to that? At least someone can use the magazines. There's piles of magazines in mom's living room, and bunches of her grandchildren. *Who'd know I was a grandma?* she'd ask. *Who'd know I was forty?* I'd say nothing: there's nothing to say. You know why she has all these children and babies. You don't know about the magazines. My mom signs the subscription cards that fly out of new magazines when you open them. She even opens magazines at the grocery store and the cards all fall out. She's not picky about what she orders—Cosmopolitan, Modern Living, Red Racing Cars, Popular Mechanics, Popular Sex Acts, Giant Redwoods, German Giants. She checks the box that says, "Bill me later." Sometimes she makes up a name a little like her name—Anna Miller, Anna Martinez, Annette Ambrosia. Not often Anita Desirado or Anita Medina. It's not always easy to remember what her real name really is.

After my mom left the supervised visitation, left the little room at the RTC and walked down the steps in her heels and walked down the street to the bus stop, my throat went tight and all the muscles in my arms grabbed hands with each other. Could I move those arms ever, ever again? They'd hang, dangle loose from my shoulders when I hurried to the third-floor bathroom, hurried as fast as I could go without grabbing, with my loose and dangling hands, the rail of the narrow, noisy stairs.

Soon enough Carlos said he was tired of bagging groceries, tired of sleeping on his sister's couch. "We could just split," he said. "Take a bus to Utah. I've got a cousin there." Carlos had plenty of cousins. I wasn't supposed to leave the state, I said. I wasn't supposed to leave Hamilton, the west side of Hamilton. "No one's going to find you in Utah," said Carlos. "No one will even look for you in Utah: it's on the other side of the continent, almost." What about my mom?

I thought, but I said nothing. My mom had missed the last three visitations— for all I knew, she'd run off to Utah herself.

In Utah, I was often cold and lonely. I couldn't cry, not even when I was afraid, and I was afraid in the morning when Carlos was sleeping, and during the day, every day, when I was supposed to look for a job. In the morning at Alberto's house, I sat there cold and afraid, watching the sun move up through the wobbling leaves of the tree across the street, waiting for it to warm up the room. I didn't really like watching the sun, but there was nothing else to watch—no TV because Alberto and Maria didn't have one yet. They were going to rent one, once he got a raise from the cardboard box factory.

The sun would be coming up pink or yellow, not blue, like the blue glass sun hung on the wall in my mom's bathroom. I was scared of that sun whose face was deep blue glass, and whose rays were twisted bronze rods. Mom's friend Paulette gave her the sun when we lived in Seattle. I was little then. Now, I wanted to see my mom, and not sit on that smelly old couch, watching a pink sun turn yellow. I wanted my mom to take care of me, even if my mom isn't the take-care-of-you type. I wanted to see Manuel, but I'd heard nothing from him, even though I'd sent a postcard to Fernando days ago now. "Let me know where you are," he said that day he appeared outside the RTC; he was there and then he was gone and I couldn't even touch him. Now I wanted to go home—wherever that was, but I couldn't go back to Hamilton, because he'd never dare find me there, and I'd just end up somewhere worse than the RTC. Probably the detention center again. I was there, last time, from December to March and I swore I'd never ever go there again.

When the sun was up to the top of the tree, the children would wander out in their pajamas, with their dirty bears and their snotty noses. Sometimes I'd get some toilet paper: Ileana let me wipe her nose, but Robert would pull away, smearing the snot even more across his face. Just a few minutes later, Renata would come in to pour the cereal. She'd ask me, always, if I'd like some cereal. Most of the time I'd say no. I didn't like to eat up their food. She's good with the kids, Renata. She sits at the table talking to them while they eat—Ileana in her booster seat, Robert on her lap. She's grinning when Robert dribbles his Cheerios on the table, not rushing around, wiping off the table, the counter, like my mom, rinsing the dishes clean. After a few minutes I'd say I had to head out. I had a lead on a job, a lead from yesterday. I tried not to say that every day. I grabbed my green sweatshirt before I left the house and didn't even think about my coat that was, for sure, not waiting anymore on that bed in Hamilton. Every day it got warm a little faster than the day before. After a while I did start walking into stores, asking for the manager, asking for job applications, but I was nervous, filling out forms, trying to make up stuff—previous employment, references—what did they know? I worked at McDonald's on East Colfax, I said, Elmer's Cleaners in Hamilton. There must be four or five McDonald's on East Colfax, and I remember the sign for the cleaners at Ninth Street and Green Ave in Hamilton. Exciting names they give those streets. The cleaners is only a block from Lincoln Park and the courthouse.

Before they sent me to the detention center, the hearing started like any other hearing in the basement of the County Court building—it was in a room without windows, with white cinder block walls and portable partitions, with the folding chairs set up in rows on the rug. My mom was there in her blue dress, with her hair pulled back, with just a little pink lipstick; she was looking polite, looking quiet, looking like a mom, not looking like my mom. My sister, Nora, sat next to my mom. When, in a robe, the lady judge came in, everyone stood up. The probation lady spoke. There were red flags in the home, she said. That sounded silly to me: we have no flags in our home—not red ones or green. The victim was in the home, she said, the brother, at least, not anymore. Not anymore because Manuel was in detention, not for the first time. She said he was being sent to the Colorado Boys Ranch. She said Marcella wasn't living up to the conditions of probation: after being expelled for fighting in seventh grade, she'd been, in ninth grade, suspended a couple of times, and she needed a lot of extra care, and she'd missed five sessions. Not that many, I thought. I couldn't have missed five.

I thought they'd probably assign me to my mom again and give her and me a list of things to do. I never thought they'd put me in detention. The court agrees with the DA, said the judge. Then the guard came from the side of the room—he put a bracelet on my wrist, put on handcuffs. He took me away, through one door, and my mom didn't come or my sister. There was different door for them.

It was the worst time—when I was in detention. After months they moved me up to the RTC. That was bad, then not so bad, but you just know, after a while, you're going to be on the run again.

One afternoon at the end of May, I just walked out of that old school, and instead of going west toward the RTC, toward the sad and heavy mountains, I crossed Apache with all the other students, hiked along 17th Street under the new leaves, crossed Shady Gulch, and met Carlos at the bus station. I had my old backpack with me—some underclothes and socks, a couple of tee shirts, a sweater. I had planned on carrying my coat, my heavy old coat, but for once it was warm, and I couldn't take any teasing at school, not that day at school: "Getting ready for Christmas, Marcella?" "There's the kid with all her clothes on her back." That morning I'd left my coat, warm and huddled, on the end of my bed.

At the Denver bus station, I was cold, and I was sure they knew at the RTC that I was on the run. They'd be onto it at dinner, and they'd be certain well before bed check. I had been at the RTC for three months, after detention. You have to do well at detention to move on up to the RTC. At detention, I did what you're supposed to, and for most of those three months at the RTC I did all right, but, after all, things can only carry on like that for just a little way. Andrea was about to learn I'd been skipping Spanish and math almost every day for the last week or two, and in Language Arts, the zero on my oral report must have wrecked my grade.

Before I ran, just before I ran with Carlos, I saw Manuel—really, I did. I was lying in the back yard of the RTC, in the sun. Someone was whispering in the bushes. I thought it would be Carlos; then I thought I was dreaming. It was Manuel's dark face in the high bushes beyond the fence—his eyes were large, his hair greasy, he was only there for a minute or two. He promised I would see him again, he promised, but I was afraid in that bus station that he didn't really mean it.

I am afraid of some things—you wouldn't think so, because I have to act, all the time, not afraid. I stand up straight, smile a little, stretch out my fingers, smile a little more. A lady asked me once—it was a counselor or a therapist or a lady. "What are you afraid of?" she asked. I didn't think I would answer.

"Going to my mom's house, my mom isn't there. Going to my mom's house, and my mom is there. Getting raped. Those girls laughing at me."

"What is the worst? Can you think about that one?"

"You have to tell me."

Maybe it wasn't the worst, but I wasn't about to speak in front of girls who used to be my friends. Anyways, they used to say they were my friends.

The week before I ran off with Carlos, on the day of the oral presentation, I just went to the media center after lunch when it was time for Language Arts. I was doing well in LA, I almost had a B, and I was prepared for the presentation after all the research I'd done on Gabriela Mistral, but after lunch I couldn't walk up the wide stairs and down the dark hall to stand in front of those girls in Language Arts who would flash half-smiles, who would giggle. You couldn't make me, Mr. Siemens couldn't make me. You might say I was afraid.

The loudspeaker was loud. It said the 10:45 to Salt Lake City and Reno would leave from Lane Three. I wasn't sure I heard the announcement; I wasn't sure that that was, finally, our bus, and I knew I could never find Lane Three. Carlos led me or pushed me onto the bus. Two policemen walked by, and they didn't look at me—maybe no one had notified security at the bus station, maybe they just didn't notice me. From the window of the bus, I could see the policemen drinking coffee; they couldn't see me.

That Tuesday, when I was supposed to give the oral report, I hung out in the media center because they never notice you, as long as you keep busy. I carried books over to the table by the computer center, skipped from one website to another. I looked up rhesus monkeys and the language of Albania, and Mr. Siemens came and found me after class. He was nice, but he said I had to give the report up in front of the class to receive a grade. I could not do that. I chose to receive a zero, and that was not good for my Language Arts grade. Maybe I could have gotten a B, but it was my choice, wasn't it?

We didn't get to Salt Lake until late the next morning. How can you sit so long in one seat? I tried to sleep—I saw Carlos asleep, leaning toward me, and he didn't look at all like Manuel. That last time I saw him, Manuel's eyes came out of the bushes, and his voice was a loud whisper—too loud for a whisper. He was on the run from detention—he was free, and it was then that I knew I'd go with Carlos. I wasn't going to hang around the RTC while Manuel was free. Write to his friend Fernando, Manuel hissed at me, write to 11 Union Street and let Fernando know where I ended up. Manuel would be in touch with Fernando. "When the heat's off, I can come get you."

In the early morning, when I left Renata's and Alberto's house, I'd go to the shopping center nearby. It's just a bit more than a strip mall—a little grass, a few benches, a little fountain that runs once in a while. I'd sit on the stone bench next to the fountain. I watched the water and watched to see if any police strolled by. I didn't see any, not on the first day or the next. On my third or fourth or seventh day there, the sun grew warm and warmer, and after a while, I took off my sweatshirt. After a while, I stopped sitting on the stone bench and went over to the straggling petunias where I was sick. Some fertilizer for the feeble flowers. I needed to eat something—then maybe I'd have energy to find a job: a job would be a good thing. Of course, it wasn't the first time I was scared about being pregnant. The first time, I hadn't even had my period yet. Then, I never got sick, but all the time, especially late in the morning and early in the afternoon, I always thought I was going to get sick. Of course, I never told Manuel or Mom, or Christine or anyone. If you tell my cousin Christine, you might as well tell everyone. A long time ago, I thought you couldn't get pregnant until after you get your period, but in seventh grade sex ed they did a good job scaring us. By the time I got out of that class, I thought you could get pregnant by eating the heads of young dandelions, by wishing on the wrong star. I was pretty young then, and after a while, I did get my period, and it was bloody, and my body was full of cramps. I had to wear a pad that felt like a rope and leaked on the edge of my underpants. One good thing about being pregnant, I thought. Then, you don't get your period for nine months.

When the movie theater opened, I went back and asked about my application. The man was short and dumpy, dumpy and jumpy, with brown hair and a large nose. He smiled when he talked to me, and some people don't look any better when they smile. His shoulders would jerk down when he stopped talking. I said my name was Maria Martinez, and I'd turned in an application more than a week ago. He went into the back and flipped through some papers. When he came back, he said, "Maria, you've come at the right time." I could feel the smell of old popcorn sneaking toward me and the dull cloud of stale and sticky floors. He told me to come back at noon for an interview. I nodded and went back out, through the heavy door. I didn't want to wait inside, looking eager, and I didn't want to smell those sticky floors.

I went out and circled the fountain, then moved further away—in case that jumpy man looked out the tall glass door. I crossed the street and walked all around the block. When I got back, it wasn't even eleven according to the clock by the bank. Maybe if I walked very slowly around the block again, I could get that clock to move. Only, I was hungry, too hungry to walk on around the block. I was watching the slow clock beside the bank, thinking someday I'd get a job in a bank, knowing I'd never get such a job, when I had an idea. I crossed at the crosswalk, stepped into that bank and came out with three lollipops—one lemon, one orange, and a brown one, probably root beer. I sucked on the lemon one first, and my whole body shivered when the first sour-sweet taste of lollipop hit my tongue. To work in a bank, of course, you have to have clothes, nice clothes. It will be a very long time before I ever have nice clothes.

During the interview, we were in a plain room without windows, and I was calm, and I was talking sweetly to a woman in a red dress and a man in a suit. There was a flat, sticky taste in my dry mouth because I'd finished all three lollipops and taken a lot of slow breaths before I went in. They asked me questions, they didn't ask how old I was. Maybe they didn't want to know. After some time talking, maybe ten minutes, or maybe twenty, they told me to go out. When they brought me back in, both grownups were standing, smiling; both shook my hand. To start, I would be sweeping the theaters and cleaning the restrooms. I'd move up, if things worked out: after a while, I could take tickets part time, maybe sell popcorn. I said that sounds great. Especially—I didn't say—the popcorn part. They told me I'd start tomorrow.

That afternoon, after I got back to the house on Peach Tree Court, Alberto came into the living room and said it was time that Carlos and I found our own place to live. We could stay a little longer while we looked, but we'd have to pay rent for those days. Carlos wasn't back yet, and Renata was standing by the stove, holding the littlest baby. She was pulling her fingers thorough his hair, careful not to look at Alberto or me.

"Okay," I said, and I didn't say I got a job. Inside me was a cold and heavy stone bench where my stomach used to be, where the baby was supposed be. We were homeless now; really, we were. For an apartment, we'd need rent and a damage deposit and we'd never get that money—even with my job. Would we live on the street? Which street? It was funny because, scared as I was, I felt relieved, almost glad. When Carlos got home, late, I told him what Alberto said. Fine by me, Carlos said. I told him I got a job and he said, "How much you going to make?" I didn't answer, at first—it was because I forgot to ask. Then I said, maybe minimum wage. Carlos said, "Hmmm, minimum wage." He said something like that again, with a swear word inside.

"Where will we go?" I asked.

He looked at me. "Where will *we* go? I got some friends I met out at the Elephant's Ear. I can go ahead and hang out with them. You find a place—it's time you got your own place."

I said nothing for a minute, but I looked scared. He said, "I think you should be glad. You should be glad you're moving along."

I'd looked for a job and I'd finally got a job, and now I was just going to start looking for something again—on my own, without any money? Right now, I could cry or get angry. In front of Carlos tonight, I was not going to cry.

"You told me to come with you. You told me to get a job. I did that and I did that and now you're pushing me out?"

He smiled. He sat down on the one chair beside the couch. It was a dusty chair, green once, a long time ago. I jumped on him and started pounding his shoulder and chest. When I pulled his light and curly hair he threw me off. Guys can't stand it if you pull at their hair. They can't even stand it when you comb their hair and hit a snarl. He stood over me, and for a moment I thought he was going to kick me. Then he did kick me. He was sorry, I think, that he did, because then he said, "Get out."

I wasn't angry anymore. I wanted to be angry, but I was just hurting so much. Still, I had to do something, so I shrieked as loud as I could, and Alberto came and Renata with the phone and only a few minutes later lights from the cops' cars were flashing on the living room walls. I was lying on the floor still and sobbing when the cops came in. They took a statement from Alberto and one from Renata. Carlos didn't say much, and I tried, but my words didn't make much sense to the cops, I could tell. They took us in their cars, in different cars, which was just as well, right then, since sitting on a back seat next to Carlos wouldn't be a good idea for me. In a little while, I was in a room with fluorescent lights, then in another room. I had no ID, so they took my picture and they took my fingerprints and asked me questions. All night they asked questions, one person after another. I'd been through this before: twice I was caught after I ran, once I turned myself in. I told the cops my name was Maria Martinez and I lived in Salt Lake. When someone touched me, I winced and tried to straighten up. I got a job, I said. I have to be there tomorrow at one. An old police guy grunted, and I knew I was going to be sick. What can you do in a room with cops, mostly men, and your hands are cuffed and you don't know where the bathroom is? I lurched toward a wastebasket and almost fell inside. I tried to kneel down, to get my balance and all the sick was hurtling through me. Most of it made its way into the basket, lucky I didn't follow it. When I'd finished being sick, I just fell onto the floor beside the basket; I couldn't make myself get up again. I had pain and no strength—my back hurt where Carlos had kicked me. Right then there was only one thing good: he was not in the room, or anywhere near. I saw Carlos last when he got out of his police car and walked ahead of me toward the police station. He was kicking at a pebble in the dark parking lot. I heard it *ping* against a light post. After he went in through the heavy door, I didn't see him again.

When a man and a lady cop stood me up and watched me hobble back to the chair, the man cop asked if I was hurt. I said it hurt on my back where Carlos kicked me.

They started asking why I got sick, and I thought it was a stupid question—anything can make you sick. I said I had no idea why, and then I was in a cop car again. That didn't make my back feel any better. At the hospital I peed in a cup, I put on the blue paper gown in the cold white room, I let cold fingers touch me. The doctor, who was young and pale and had pale, thin hair, asked memorized questions. I answered politely. Was my back hurting now? Yes. Did I know I was pregnant? Yes. How long? How long? How long did I know? How long had I been pregnant? How long? He said I wasn't so very far along—had I been considering termination? I stopped answering politely, I stopped answering. While the doctor talked to a policewoman in the corner, a nurse brought in a couple of pills. "These will help with the pain—and don't worry: they won't hurt your baby. I'll see if I can get you a scrip for when you go."

For a long time I was alone in the room—I wanted my mom, I wanted Manuel. Would they ever let me go home? But now I was Maria Martinez. Did she even have a home? When the pills began to work, I didn't feel so lonely. Can you sleep on a narrow examining table with a slippery paper cover? I was about to find out when the police came in again. I was going to detention, and there would be a hearing tomorrow.

I was on a bus back to Denver when my pain pills ran out. Then, my back hurt as much as ever and I wanted to be sick, all the time. On one side of me sat a lady cop, mostly looking straight ahead. She didn't even open a magazine to read. On the other side was a man cop who tried to talk to me sometimes. Sometimes I said nothing, sometimes I said, "No." Even on the bus, they made me wear the orange pajamas I got in detention and they handcuffed my wrist to the seat arm—but there was no way I was going to run, not now. I thought of Manuel showing up at Alberto's and Renata's. "Marcella? Marcella who? Never heard of her." It was a long ride to Denver, and then, in a police car, a short ride to Hamilton where they put me right away in detention. I thought they'd remember me in detention, but they treated me like someone new. I guess the Marcella Medina, who was Maria Martinez for a while, a little while, was not the same person as the Marcella Medina who used to hang out here. I was an offender again, I'd be diagnosed again and, as before, effectively supervised and provided with a continuum of services. I'd be provided with programs that promote accountability to victims and build skills and competencies to become a responsible citizen. So who were the victims I was accountable to? Renata and Alberto, the RTC? No way.

A couple of mornings after I got back to Hamilton, they put me in a small room, a new room I'd never seen before. Instead of cinderblock walls painted soupy-green and a linoleum covered floor, instead of a table with a folding metal chair on one side and a folding metal chair on the other, it was a wallpapered room, a carpeted room, with, everywhere, flowers—on the couch and carpet, on the wallpaper and armchair, blooms clashing, colliding. Too much, with the flowers, I thought. The counselor, Ms. Morrissey, sat me in the middle of this overgrown garden, sat me on the ruffled armchair. She perched on the couch arm, balancing a clipboard on her knee.

Ms. Morrissey was almost young, with makeup, a lot of nice makeup, and dark hair pulled into a ponytail. She dressed like a grownup at work—wearing a white blouse, a dark skirt, a tight dark skirt, and high, high heels,

"Have you thought about what you'll do with the baby, Marcella?"

They were concerned, all of them, with the baby, although from what I knew it was going to be months and months before there'd be any baby to worry about.

"Have you considered terminating the pregnancy, Marcella? From what I understand, that is a definite option one might consider. You aren't so very far along."

"Maybe you've contemplated placing the baby with an adoptive family? Once you've completed your time in detention, we could find you a home, a place to stay until the birth, until the relinquishment."

I looked at her right shoulder. I didn't bother to speak.

"Is the father in the picture? There's always the relinquishment papers to think about."

Carlos, not Carlos. No. He's not in any picture I know about, not anymore.

The next time I met the counselor, she asked about my mother, my brother. I noticed the small buds on the couch were a different color than the large flowers.

"When you were growing up, Marcella, was your mother in the home a good deal of the time?"

"And your brother, your older brother, did he live there as well?"

I answered, just a little, just enough so she'd know I could speak. I looked at her plain shoulder, at the flowery wallpaper. My mom was at home, of course, when she wasn't working. My brother lived there, and my other brother and my sisters and my cousin and I lived with my mom, most of the time. Where else would we live?

"Most of the time?"

We'd stayed with Christine's mother once, for a couple of weeks. That was not a very good time. I didn't want to talk about it. I didn't talk about it.

The third time I met with the counselor, she said my mom was coming in, if that was all right.

Did she mean I had a choice about seeing my mom? Did she think I didn't want to see my mom? I looked surprised, and I nodded. What else would you do?

I waited. I watched the flowers fade on the wallpaper; soon they'd be drying, petals drifting with a dusty smell, down to litter the pale carpet. I wondered—if my mom came in, where would she sit? I was in the armchair, Ms. Morrissey on one end of the couch. If my mom sat on the other end of the couch, how would the counselor talk to her—over her left shoulder, twisting and turning each time, awkwardly, uncomfortably? Would my mom even come in? Ms. Morrissey might not know my mom's record when it came to attending meetings. I glanced at the door, once and then again while

Ms. Morrissey pressed her questions on me. Would my mom even come? Would she wear a dress spread with bright flowers?

And she came after a while, after I'd quite given up and had begun to listen to the questions. She came in a blue and white striped dress, with a tan on her face and fine wrinkles on her tan; she came over to me, as if to hug me. I watched in surprise, till I realized the hugging was for the counselor's sake. I stood stiffly inside her circling arms. I smelled sweet powder, I wanted to cough. This was my mom, this old lady? I sat again, my bum squashing the blossoms on the armchair.

My mom looked round and around the room, a little awkward, a little confused, then she balanced on the edge of the cushion, on the far end of the couch. Ms. Morrissey turned awkwardly; they talked uncomfortably. Ms. Morrissey asked about my childhood. Mom admired the upholstery and the wallpaper. It was a normal enough childhood, I guess. The counselor mentioned the violence in the home, the exposure to sexual activities, the sexual activities. My mom admired my new shoes. It was a normal enough childhood, I guess.

Ms. Morrissey presented, as she saw it, options for my future. One was continued detention. One was a place at Mrs. Collins's, even after the baby was born. Mutual-care foster home, it was called.

I wanted to swing my legs like a child, but my legs were too long. They crumbled down over my sad feet in their stiff new shoes.

"Have you heard about your brother?" That was my mom's voice pitched too high. The sounds rose, circled the moon, landed back on my lap, wetting my lap.

"Which brother?" There were two, anyway, three if you counted Luis who was a half-brother, but never a part of our family.

"Manuel, of course. You know I mean Manuel." She was looking straight at me, my mom, with eyes sharp as a fly's eyes, with her teeth scraping, pulling off the bright lipstick on her lower lip, looking as if she knew the news would bother me, as if she were not sorry it would.

"Manuel has a beard now," she said. "Can you imagine? It's a scrawny beard, kind of wispy. Enough of one so that Alvaro mentioned it to Luis and Luis told Fernando. So he wants to be a grownup, our Manuel."

She was smiling, our mom, and I was smiling—how much I wanted to see that gaunt face decorated with a few black wisps. But she worried me. She was talking about Manuel and he was on the run—how could she talk about Manuel in front of a counselor in a flowery room?

She said Manuel had a girl. "She's called Isabella, his girl, his new girl; she has long hair, dark and long, down past her waist, and already, he's knocked her up. Last I heard, they're on their way to California, or maybe Arizona. Maybe he's going to get married—that's what they say."

"Stop! Stop!" I was screaming at her. "How do you know? You can't know about Manuel's life in hiding. You know they'll say anything when a kid's on the run."

"Oh, grow up, Marcella. You think Manuel's going to act, forever, like a boy at home? He's out in the world and he's going to act like boys do, out in the world. What happens, happens. Look at you: you're going to have a baby. You think you're the only one?"

The morning before I woke from a dream of Manuel. In the dream I saw him sleeping and opened him and read these stories like stories in a book. You have to know, these are only leaves of a book, only words on the leaves. I woke from the dream, and I was in the cell in detention. The other girl was still asleep. How could she sleep?

It was later, in that flowery room, after they'd taken my mom out, after I'd stopped screaming and just huddled in the armchair, my shoes kicked off, my toes tucked under me, later, when Ms. Morrissey had come back in and said, "Well, Marcella," that I told her, my voice in a soft, sad whisper, that I'd go to Mrs. Collins's house, to the mutual care home—if that could be arranged. I said I'd go there and wait for the baby to be born, but it was going to be my baby; this baby wasn't going to be handed off to anyone else.

"That sounds like a plan, Marcella. You know, first, there will be a hearing."

"I know," I said, "I know." Always, there is a hearing, I know. And I knew for a few weeks, or months, in the mutual care home, I'd pull my hair back into a ponytail and do what I was told. After a few weeks, or months, they would trust me. After that, not long after that, it would be easy enough to be on the run again.

HORIZONTAL HOLD

On Tuesday night when I walked down the basement steps to my room, a dog was crying across the park, and the upstairs light went out. The upstairs light went out, and my light was out, but the television was on. My light bulb and the television are on timers to confuse the intruders when I am not home. They could confuse the intruders when I am there as well, and usually, if my bus driver doesn't forget to take off his sunglasses when the streetlights come on, I am home by 11:30 at night.

I never make it home until 11:30 because I work as a janitor at the Francis Stoddard Elementary School, and I begin work, most days, after the children have tripped onto the school bus, although before the teachers have stopped gossiping in the lounge. At 10:30 on Tuesday night I'd extracted some valuables from the trash bin and had rolled the last load of trash to the dumpster behind the kitchen. When I'd dumped the afternoon's accumulation of crayon shavings, paper porcupines, bloody scissor halves, and cherry roll-up wrappings, I pushed the bin back to the door. Then I put the doorstop, my sneaker, back on my foot, went inside, and slid the bin to its closet inside, to its place beside the brooms and mops. On Tuesday evening I made it back into the building without incident, but when I had first started work as the janitor, I locked myself out of the school every night for two weeks; it took me that long to think of propping the back door open with my sneaker. Those first two weeks, each night, I had to walk around the building and unlock the front door. I had a key to the front door.

On Tuesday night before leaving school, I'd secured the various valuables I'd collected—unsharpened pencils, broken reading glasses from the assistant principal's desk, a couple of half-eaten apples, and so on—in my backpack. I turned off the main switch of the building, checked to be sure the front door locked behind me, and caught the 11:02 bus. The windows of the house where I lived went dark as the people upstairs watched my return across the park.

In the basement, by the light of the old television, I located the bottle of scotch beneath the sink, and I watched the TV movie, drinking from the pink chipped cup. It was a murder movie, not old like my TV, but set in olden times. The women wore pretty long skirts; the men wore thin mustaches and hair parted in the middle.

Mrs. Samuelson, a witness in the murder trial, was playing with her pocketbook; I could hear it click. Almost. The camera shifted from the witness to the defendant, to the witness, to the jury. The cameraman couldn't make up his mind. The defendant, because of nervousness or because of egg yolk, used his little fingernail to comb the left corner of his mustache.

Yes, the witness had seen the defendant with the deceased. Click. She had seen that man with the girl on the front steps of the factory, on the steps of the Atlanta Pencil Factory.

The screen blurred, then it dimmed to a fuzzy-edged flashback; life grew easier for the nervous cameraman. On the stone steps of the pencil factory the defendant was talking to the victim. Leonard Judd, sad and thin, looked at the young girl and he smiled, and as he smiled, he seemed to remember another girl on another staircase. Leonard Judd's shoulders were set back on a broomstick behind his head, and when he leaned toward the girl, saying "Hello Rosa," his head bobbed like a turtle's. The girl did not look at the man; she looked at her foot as it slid along the step, back and forth, catching the dip of the stone. There were dips, foot-worn, on each step. When it rained, a chain of small puddles would climb the steps. With her pocketbook Mrs. Samuelson climbed the steps slowly, her wide body turned sideways. She managed to skirt the couple, but she ran into the fuzzies at the edge of the screen. The girl's braids, Rosa Fleming's braids, fell forward and swung beside her face; Leonard Judd's little finger came up to scratch his mustache.

The fuzzies faded; the picture sharpened, and the courtroom returned. The next witness, the office boy, came to the stand. The office boy, Casey Mann, not quite a man, grinned at Leonard Judd and winked at the camera. Casey had gray skin, a lopsided bow tie, and he tried hard to listen as the prosecutor posed the questions. Casey had gray skin because I had a black and white TV. Everyone in the movie, in every movie, had gray skin, too.

When he worked, said Casey, most of the time he sharpened pencils. He liked sharp pencils and he liked to test the pencil points on his finger. Then, with his knife, he would whittle the pencil sharper, then he would test it against his finger again. Casey's damaged finger ran round and around the rim of his jacket button. The prosecutor asked a question, and Casey's mouth stayed open.

Yes. When he ran down to the first floor with a message for the foreman, he saw someone on the stairs with Rosa Fleming. He remembered that Rosa Fleming. He remembered he would like to poke her with a pencil.

He had thought she was laughing—she could have been screaming. That man she was with, he could have been Leonard Judd. It was dark. Yes, there was a window above the stairs, but it didn't give much light. He delivered the message to the factory foreman, Casey said, and he went back upstairs. There could have been a man on the stairs when he went back up. It could have been Leonard Judd carrying that girl. Could have been, maybe. There are other tall guys around, you know—the foreman's assistant, the supervisor, the janitor. The guy on the stairs said something. No. Casey didn't remember what the guy said. The next thing he remembered was when the police were in the building. Well yes, that was the next day. It was, anyway, the next thing he remembered.

Casey's mouth gaped during the defense attorney's cross-examination, and his lower jaw remained open; the television went off.

As I did most nights, I sat and watched the screen while it remained gray in the dark room. For five or seven minutes longer, I watched the screen. I watched it until shapes appeared in the room—the curved couch arm, the straight edge of the shade. I wouldn't pull up the shade. I knew if I did, the streetlight would fall into my basement room and blind me. I watched the gray screen, and I didn't try to figure out what, in the movie, had already happened, or what would happen next. They run these movies day after day at different times, over and over, as if we don't have anything better to do than watch the same movies over and over. In a week or two, I knew, the whole movie with variations would run through my time slot. Some nights, after the movie goes off, my days with variations run on the blank screen, and some nights the light bulb turns on, and the children upstairs scream.

On Tuesday evening I stared at the screen and tried to figure out who Casey Mann reminded me of. That afternoon, after school, I'd watched a scene in the principal's office as I dusted the big desk and rearranged the names in the Rolodex. Over the years I've watched plenty of scenes in the principal's office. Whoever notices the janitor? I'm there; the furniture is there. What's the difference? There were a few teachers in the office along with the principal. And there was a kid held after, a kid standing with his mouth open in front of the principal's desk. That was Oskar Primos, a fifth grader, and he was the kid Casey Mann reminded me of. Oskar had orange hair, a copper earring, and he stood in the office with his pink mouth slightly ajar, with the peaks of his hair drooping slightly. Oskar is the sort of kid that principals, other kids, and teachers all don't like. Oskar had folded the cuff of his white sleeve, and he pushed the sleeve again and again, up above his elbow. Again and again the sleeve slid down. Finally, Oskar folded the sleeve above his elbow and the pink arm dangled from the uncomfortable roll of cloth as if it were attached to the shirt, not the shoulder.

On Tuesday afternoon in the principal's office, I found out why Oskar was held after. I learned that the kids, the principal, and the teachers had all decided that Oskar was the one who beat up a second grader after school. He left him near the dumpster, on the blacktop. Oskar had stayed late at school finishing his math assignment in the fifth-grade classroom, before he left around four. Not long after, one of the teachers said, some mom picking up a Girl Scout found a second-grade boy limping across the parking lot. She helped him to the principal's office. She found Jason Mackerel on Monday afternoon, and his curly hair was matted with mud and canned peas. I knew that little kid. He had curly hair but a flat face. No rosy cheeks.

I knew what they were talking about. Of course I couldn't say anything as I emptied the pencil sharpener. After all, you know, a janitor is not much more than furniture. No reason to remind anyone.

I knew when school was out on Monday, Jason Mackerel, the second grader, came back to school as he did most days, to ride his bicycle on the sidewalks and on the blacktop of the playground. Jason Mackerel was still riding his bike when the Girl Scout meeting let out at 4:30. I knew when the Girl Scout meeting let out because that was when I'd meet Angela Morris, another sixth grader. They would come out of the side door, those green girls, when I was taking out the first load of trash. After a while, on Mondays, I would take out the trash a little later, and Angela would hang behind the other girls. She had yellow hair, two holes in each ear, a prim smile, an earring in one of the holes. Did she think the other green girls didn't figure out she was meeting the janitor, figure out she was meeting me? I wondered. Did she care? Not likely she cared.

On Monday the bicycle wheel was turning, and its frame lay on the ground when I stood with one hand on the trash bin and one hand holding the door. Jason Mackerel lay on the ground and his hands were over his cap, over his head. Two sixth-grade boys were holding him down while Angela Morris kicked his back and his shoulder with her pointy little boots, and there were splashes of dirt on her white tights. The sixth graders looked alarmed, just slightly alarmed, when they spotted me. They took off and Angela turned toward me and sneered.

"This little fucker's been watching us," she said. "He was squatting down there at the corner, waiting for us."

I didn't let the kitchen door close.

Her eyes narrowed to slits as she watched me. Then she smiled; it was not a prim smile. "You tell on me, garbage man, I'll tell on you." She slapped the dumpster. "We could just dump it in there. Why not. Destroy the evidence. Why not."

Jason Mackerel was beginning to crawl away. Angela gouged his butt with her boot. I was kind of sorry for the kid. He used the dumpster to pull himself up.

I stepped back inside the kitchen door and let it close behind me.

"He was in pretty bad shape," the principal told the teachers the next afternoon, Tuesday afternoon. "That little second grader, Jason Mackerel, was pretty beat up, yesterday, when he stood by my desk. 'Could have been one guy,' he said. 'Could have been two guys,' he decided."

"He couldn't see," the principal told the teachers. "He couldn't see because they pulled his hat down over his face and tied it with his scarf. He couldn't see much anyhow because he had his hands over his face most of the time when they were kicking him. He thought he saw an earring, maybe a pointy boot."

"You know," the principal told Oskar in the principal's office, "There's not much doubt because of the earring. You, Oskar Primos, are the only fifth- or sixth-grade boy with an earring."

"It wasn't me, not me," cried Oskar. "I bet it was those other guys. Not me. No, I dint! Who says? You know who it was? Those big guys. The big guys in sixth grade."

The principal said something about overwhelming circumstantial evidence, but the lack of definitive proof. "Make no mistake, young man; we will be keeping a close eye on you."

And it was Oskar Primos who resembled Casey Mann, the office boy on the witness stand. They looked like they were asleep during the joke and that they woke up too late for the punch line. They were not quite the same. Casey had no shadows on his arms, and he had sick, gray skin. Oskar had freckled skin, and, I'm sure, when he was sleeping, his little sister, or cockroaches, got into the Vaseline and fucked around with his orange hair. The hair of the kid on TV was not orange; prematurely, it was gray.

When the TV light gave out, I stood and stumbled on the stuffing that fell from the couch cushions. I landed on the couch and slept there. It smelled of stale bagels, hair grease, and dried ants. I didn't particularly like the smell, but it was, at least, familiar.

On Wednesday the TV came on as I ate my dinner. I ate Vienna sausages that looked like children's fingers and tasted like the aluminum can. I drank pink whiskey that tasted like gasoline. On Wednesday, on the TV, black vertical lines intersected with diagonal slashes and the horizontal hold did not hold.

The janitor of the pencil factory flipped by. He was large, growing larger. His chin rose toward the top of the screen and his forehead appeared on his chest. The janitor, Jerry Cornwall, broke a handful of pencils, and the wastebasket rose to the top of the screen. Jerry Cornwall dumped the wastebasket into a large bin full of shavings. The stairs of the pencil factory flipped by. Jerry Cornwall, slowly, stumbling, carried a body down the stairs.

During the commercial I thought of other janitors and other kids. At Francis Stoddard Elementary, where I work, the janitor makes doorstops out of sneakers; the first graders and kindergartners carry teddy bears and toy trucks up the steps of the elementary school on Show and Tell day. During inside recess, when it rains, they build small castles with their pencils.

On the TV, boxes of pencils in stacks flipped by, and one stack was not as high as the others. Leonard Judd, the factory superintendent, flipped by. He rearranged the stacks to make them even, and as he gave the last stack a satisfied pat, the police walked in. They charged him with the murder of Rosa Fleming, and Leonard Judd adjusted his bow tie.

The horizontal hold did not hold.

A while later, not a short while later, the judge spoke in long sentences with long pauses, and he spoke in sober tones. The judge stared at the jury, the camera stared at the jury, and the jury squirmed. During the long pauses the judge would pull out the knob of his watch; he would spin the knob, changing the watch hands, and then he'd push the knob in again. Either the judge thought he could rearrange the position of the sun, or he enjoyed the sound of the click. The judge, making use of his long sentences, handed down the sentence. For the murder of Rosa Fleming, Leonard Judd was to hang.

The jury, satisfied, stopped squirming. Rosa Fleming's mother wove her gray handkerchief in and out of her thick fingers and stared at the blank wall between the judge's head and the empty witness stand. The judge stared at Leonard Judd; the camera stared at Leonard Judd; Jerry Cornwall, the janitor, stared at Leonard Judd and shook his head slowly. Leonard Judd licked his mustache and looked at a pencil on the table.

When the TV went off on Wednesday, I took a sip of nothing from my empty cup, frowned at the staring screen, and considered the taste of the tiled walls in the boys' john at Francis Stoddard. That afternoon there were three sixth graders in the john when I went in to empty the trash. The one who pushed in ahead of me was a kid I'd seen hanging around with Angela Morris. On Wednesday the john was bright and smoky. Its yellow walls smelled, but they smelled worse when they were wet. The walls were wet on Fridays when I scrubbed the graffiti that was too boring to read any more. On Wednesday the sixth graders complained about Oskar. "He told on us, he did. That tattletale—we gotta get him." The john didn't smell too bad on Wednesday because the kids smoked pot as they conspired to get Oskar, as they dropped their underwear on the floor. On my way out I turned on the hot water and turned off the lights. I thought those kids led such exciting lives.

On Thursday night I came the long way home from the bus stop. While the short way was just across the street and up the alley, the long way was up two blocks and through the park. In the park I had to set each swing ajar, slide down the slide, cross over the jungle gym, and swing across the monkey bars, wearing my backpack the whole way. If I missed a swing, or if I dropped from the monkey bars, part-way across, I had to start over.

On Thursday I made it, tired as I was. When I got to the house, it was quiet upstairs and there was a smell of burnt margarine. When the TV came on, I drank a glass of orange juice. It tasted of copper.

On Wednesday the judge had sentenced Leonard Judd to die.

On Thursday the judge sentenced Leonard Judd to die, and the governor commuted the sentence, and the crowd gathered on the courthouse lawn.

I fell asleep watching the TV, and it was off when I woke. I was still tired. It seemed I'd been at the Francis Stoddard Elementary School for a week and a half or a year and a half. I couldn't leave until after I'd cleaned the kindergarten and vacuumed all the carpets, after I'd watched the playground through the ammonia and crayon on the fourth-grade window, after I'd folded the cafeteria tables and swept the cafeteria and gathered the trash.

On the other side of the fourth-grade window, on the other side of the playground, I'd watched as the sixth graders played by the backstop. The game had started out as a baseball game after school, but the baseball kept disappearing in the long grass beside the playground. After a while, the boys started passing the bat around, and the game was more like fox and geese than baseball. It was more like foxes and goose, and the goose was always Oskar Primos, the fifth grader with the orange hair. They kept going after him with the bat. He would laugh and run and flash the bird and slip in the mud. He was fast, but he fell a lot and then the one with the bat, whoever had the bat, would get him. In a couple of days his bruises would resemble the second-grade sink after finger painting, or the sides of the cafeteria garbage can at noon. I saw Angela Morris cheering from the bleachers, and Oskar, limp, curled on the ground. Then Angela was cheering from behind the backstop. Her fingers grabbed the webs of the backstop. I didn't see what they did with the body. I had to sweep the cafeteria and sweep the gym. Before dumping the trash and catching the bus, I had to lean over the side of the dumpster. In the dark I had to feel around for a body buried in the trash.

The television went off some time after I fell asleep Thursday. A while after I woke; I turned the TV back on. The sun shone on the courthouse dome. The sun reflected off the foreheads of the people listening to a man on the courthouse steps. One large hand clenched the iron railing, the other hand punched periods in the air. The railing was too thin for the wide courthouse steps, and the man's clothes were too dark for the afternoon sun. The people cheered silently; they wiped their foreheads and sprinkled sweat on the courthouse lawn, watering the grass with salt. They thrust hats in the air, but they didn't let go. Later they'd need the hats for fans.

I drank whiskey from the chipped coffee cup. The camera moved close to the crowd. A boy in the crowd ripped his comic book apart. Methodically, he shredded a page to long strips; neatly tore the strips across, carefully tucked the ragged rectangles into his overalls' front pouch. The boy tore out another page. He did not look up, but occasionally his cowlick bent to the exhortations of the crowd.

I turned up the sound. Upstairs the woman and the children cried and cried so I turned the sound up louder.

The pale, dry streets had dark patches of day-old puddles, and the man with the rope ran through the streets and ran through the puddles, and the mud on his shoes collected dust from the road. The man with the rope joined the dark-suited man on the courthouse steps and they shouted brave words to the crowd. They cheered and they descended to the mob. They left their footprints on the courthouse steps. The boy in overalls sprinkled comic book confetti on the mob.

They were enjoying it. They were smiling, swinging hatchets, singing, breaking glass. One guy was happily jumping up and down. "You know, it wasn't him," he cried. "It wasn't him, it was this other guy, you know. It was the janitor!" One or two guys stopped and looked at him. They stopped looking and rejoined their mob.

Mobs charged from the opposite ends of the same street toward each other. I wondered if, converging, each would trample the other, if one or two nimble boys would be left to bounce, light-footed over the arms and backs, slipping in the sweat, catching toes on the short-sleeved arms. But the two mobs met at a brick building and both groups surged up the steps. Soon faces appeared—on the roof, at the windows. There were only a few casualties, only one or two dark rag dolls flopped from the roof or fell from the windows.

In negative, a silhouette emerged on the TV screen. The mob raged on. The shape of the hanged man appeared and grew larger: within the silhouette the mob rampaged, in negative, white eyes on black; without, the mob rampaged, black on white.

On Friday I slept late, and I barely made it to school on time. Police cars were at the school. I learned that Oskar's parents had called the school the evening before when Oskar never came home Thursday afternoon. When there was no answer, they called the police. The police arrived at Francis Stoddard Elementary School to investigate. They arrived not long after I left, and they were still investigating when I got to school on Friday around three. The teachers, at three o'clock, were relieved that they could finally let the kids go home. None of the fifth graders or second graders or any other graders had paid any attention in class with all the policemen wandering around. There was no sign of Oskar Primos at school or anywhere between school and his home. A reporter from Channel 7 attempted to interview Oskar's parents. Oskar's parents did not wish to be interviewed. No one said anything about the dumpster. I didn't ask.

On Friday evening I heated baked beans and burned them in the thin aluminum saucepan. I cut my thumb as I cut open the cellophane wrapping of the hot dog package. The TV was already on.

On Friday Casey Mann, the office boy, ran into Jerry Cornwall on the stairs. "It wasn't me, man," said Jerry Cornwall. "You know it could never have been me."

On Friday the citizens of Atlanta rolled newspapers into cones and pulled pillowcases over their heads. I sliced the hot dogs, stirred them into the baked beans, and scraped my dinner into a bowl. The mob on TV nearly lynched Jerry Cornwall. The good people of Atlanta dragged him slowly down the front steps of the pencil factory, down the street, and Casey Mann stumbled after the crowd. He was crying, the only one crying, and he never saw Jerry Cornwall pull away from his captors and run toward the top right-hand corner of the TV screen. The movie's sad music grew louder and slower as the credits slid sadly down the screen. That was it. Finally, the gloomy movie was at an end.

On Friday the mob did its best to lynch Jerry Cornwall.

On Saturday Casey Mann and the principal of Francis Stoddard Elementary School carried Rosa Fleming to the school playground.

On Saturday Jason Mackerel and Jerry Cornwall tied jump ropes around the ankles of Angela Morris and tied the jump ropes to the back of Jason's bike. They dragged Angela twice around the playground, taking turns, and left her beneath the swings.

On Sunday Leonard Judd and Jason Mackerel placed the body of Oskar Primos gently in the dumpster.

112 Months

I was thinking about two sons and separation when the cat appeared on the other side of the window, wanting to come in. It was a warm day in late winter. Behind the cat, dry stalks of last year's grasses moved stiffly in the wind. The cat has no strong feelings about my sons: he's never met one, and he's wary, if not exactly frightened, of the other. No longer does the cat hide under the bed or disappear from the room when the little boy enters it. My cat, who is orange, crouches down, and the skin tightens across his back.

I pushed open the window and thought about how long it would be before I saw my second son, who is four and named Benjamin. The cat crossed the sill onto my desk, sniffed at my coffee cup, then dropped onto the floor and left the room. Before I saw Benjamin again, I would complete the editing of one article, read a chapter or two, jot down notes for my own essay, prepare lunch and eat it, look through a grant proposal, work on a second article, locate my car keys and coat, and, finally, drive the twenty-minute drive to his school. Earlier that morning when I dropped Benjamin off at preschool just after eight, I told him it wouldn't be long until I'd see him again, but it had been long. I told him the time would pass quickly, and it did, but when I looked back later, a long time had gone by. I closed the window and tasted my cold coffee. Before I saw my cat again, I would attempt to write about two sons and separation.

When my first son, Alexander, was born, we were separated very soon after his birth. During the birth I was breathing through an oxygen mask because I had pneumonia, and the oxygen created a distance between the rest of the world and me. When I closed my eyes, sand paintings appeared; they arranged and rearranged themselves continually. When I opened my eyes, it was as if I was on the far side of a window. On the other side of the glass, people moved and appeared to talk, but they had nothing to do with me. Way down at the other end of my body, Alexander was being born, and after his birth they examined him down at the far end of the room. I did try to peer around the nurses who attended me and around the green-capped doctors examining him. I closed my eyes and sand paintings appeared. I opened my eyes and attempted to lift my head to get a glimpse of my baby. The green-garbed nurse beside me said, "Don't worry. They'll bring him over to see you before they take him to the RNICU." And they did. I saw his pink face in profile; the rest of him was bundled in green drapes. Maybe I was seeing him. Perhaps he was seeing his reflection in the glass around me. They took him away then—they had to take him away because he was nearly three months premature, and I had to remain behind to wait for my placenta to deliver—which it did not want to do. That was our first separation.

Early that morning when I had leaned over to wake Benjamin, he held his eyes closed and tried not to smile. Before opening his eyes, he asked, "Do I go to school today?" Later at my desk I clicked a button on my mechanical pencil, attempting to lengthen the lead, and thought that now Benjamin was building a tower with blocks whose paint was chipping off, or, with his heel, digging a long narrow ditch across the pebbles of the playground. Certainly, by now, he was happy. By now he'd let go of the pain of parting.

When I'd tried to leave him at preschool that morning, I said it wouldn't be long before I saw him again. I knelt down, holding him, and he was crying: "It's too long a time. It's too long. I want to go home with you." What do I do? I thought. I like holding him, I'd like to take him home, I'd like to hold him for the rest of my life. I can kneel here forever, I can keep on kneeling; but the hard floor is beginning to flatten my kneecap.

I looked up at Anna, the teacher, who, I thought, should be calm and sure, who, instead, appeared anxious. She was thinking, Now what do we do? She said, "Do you need some help?" And I let her hold Benjamin as I left. I just walked out. I don't know if he ran to the door.

I put down the pencil and picked it up again. I turned on the computer and looked out the window. Small clumps of snow, left over from a storm three days ago, weighted the ponderosa branches. How are you supposed to get anything done when you drop your child off at school and he is crying?

The pine branches were moving, shaking loose handfuls of snow. The wind had come up again. Certainly there have been times that

I've used as much energy thinking about, worrying about, Alexander as I do the other two children, but lately he's been pushed farther back—to the back of my mind, to the back of my back where he spreads between the skin and muscle.

This morning it was persistent, everyday worries about Benjamin that both evoked Alexander and forced him aside. I wanted to call the school, and I was hesitant to call. I knew what the teachers would think: *Why must you waste our time?* Or maybe not. What kind of a mother can walk away from a child and forget about him for the rest of the day? If I didn't call, clearly I'd forgotten him. If I did call, I was bothering them. In the end, I picked up the phone. While you'd rather not, you must be ready to look like a fool for your child. The phone rang four times; then the answering machine came on. I had to leave a message, but at least I'd done something, and when I'd hung up the phone, I could concentrate a little better on my work. Of course it was just for my own sake that I called.

The orange cat stretched his paws up onto the seat of my chair, demanding attention. While he likes to be near me, he rarely insists on physical attention. He does not jump onto my shoulders, as my gray cat often did; he does not lie on the computer keys. I scratched his neck while he batted at my hand. I opened the window, and he leapt onto the sill where he stood, for a minute or more, with his head stretched out toward the cold wind blowing in. I wanted to close the window. I wanted to get on with my work. My work was suspended by a cat on the windowsill, and I was growing cold. Finally, he dropped down onto the grass. Outside the crows cried.

When we were newly bereaved—that first year or two or three—a friend of mine, who had also lost her firstborn son, would remind me of the energy it took to care for a dead child. Her second son had been born a year and nine months after the birth and death of her first. She would say, "I have good reason to be so tired. After all, it's not just David that I'm caring for." I was worn out as well, caring for one, then two lively and demanding babies, and one insistent memory. But, I thought, since I no longer expend the energy each day on Alexander that I once did, and since the other two need less of my time than when they were babies, why am I still so tired?

The phone rang. It was Kathie, the director of the preschool, seven and three-quarters months pregnant herself with her first child, a boy. She said Benjamin had been upset for about three minutes after I left; then he went off to play with the trains in the brown room. He was fine now, and she'd have a little talk with him before school was over for the day.

"Maybe on Wednesday," I said, "Maybe I should stay for a while, to ease the transition. A few days ago, when I was in the waiting room at the doctor's office, I read an article about that, about boys and transitions, about easing little boys through transitions."

Kathie hesitated. The orange cat peered in the window. His mouth moved, but I couldn't hear him. Kathie said, "Of course you are welcome to stay. If it were the beginning of the year, I don't think I'd recommend it, but . . ."

When I'd hung up the phone, I felt a little better, but somewhat uneasy. Clearly she did not think my staying on Wednesday such a good idea. But then, what kind of mother are you if you can't endure some uneasiness for your child?

My first separation from Alexander did not affect me deeply: I was in some sort of shock. Twelve hours earlier, when I'd learned that my baby would soon be born, I went numb. This was not, after all, something that could actually be happening—I'd only started wearing my sister's maternity clothes a couple of weeks earlier. Twelve hours before his birth I lay in the intermediate care unit of the maternity ward where I was recovering from abdominal surgery. I had nearly three months of pregnancy ahead of me, and I wasn't thinking much about my pregnancy; I was wondering when they would let me eat again. It was the middle of the night, and three beds down from me, a very pregnant, very large woman, temporarily under observation after a bad fall, was sucking down a large strawberry milkshake, and I wanted one. I'd been on intravenous feedings for a week and a half, and I craved real food. Then one of the residents examined me. The residents performed pelvic exams as regularly as they checked my temperature, pulse, and blood pressure. But this time, instead of saying "Zero, zero," as he dropped the sheet and peeled off his gloves, Dr. Campbell said, "Two, zero." My cervix was two centimeters dilated.

No, I thought. No. You're supposed to say, "Zero, Zero." I was furious at him. Then I went numb. There was no more emotion, not until late the next afternoon.

My fever had gone up, the residents said. I probably had pneumonia, the residents said. The baby wanted to come, and they would no longer try to stop it. We have to listen to the baby, they said. When the baby was born, I was still in shock. I didn't protest when they took him away, when they put me under to perform a D and C and deliver the placenta. My mind evaporated, a separate universe superseded it; then, after a long time had gone by, a body lay on a table in a delivery room, and I came back into that body. In the recovery room I was, at least, occasionally conscious; white walls appeared, nowhere near me. Doctors leaned over—but I had no thoughts. Late that afternoon, they moved me back into the labor room, the green room without windows that had, for two and a half days, served as ICU while I recuperated from surgery, while I endured incision pain and dry mouth and the magnesium sulfate intended to stop my contractions. And now I was returned to the labor room, no longer in labor, but still, I suppose, in shock. Then my husband came in, beaming, and I surfaced. We'd had a baby, and I had to see my baby. Now.

They took me to see him, and I was amazed. This baby didn't look much like the pink profile I recalled, and although he weighed only three pounds, he didn't, then, look terribly small. He was spread on the warming table, breathing, his legs splayed out from his hips at an awkward angle. His eyes were closed, but he was not necessarily asleep. He was waiting, figuring things out, and he filled my field of vision. He filled my eyes. I had to soak him in.

When I was with my baby, I took everything in—his long jawbone, his serious demeanor, his kicks, the curve of his fingers. When I was away from him—far away, back in my room, through two sets of heavy double doors, down several long halls—I felt fiercely possessive. I understood the mother wolf who would bite and kill for her young. At the same time, curiously enough, I felt I wasn't a real mother at all. I didn't belong on the maternity ward, for, after all, I hadn't endured nine long months of pregnancy, and I didn't have a baby beside my bed. Those other mothers had babies in their rooms.

The wind let up, and I pushed the window open so that the cat could come in and out as he pleased. Right then, I didn't mind having the window open, but as soon as the wind began again, it would get cold. From behind the blue mountains to the south a gray cloud, bright at the edges, pushed up, spreading into the clear sky. A few minutes later the cat came in the window, and he seemed to tumble slightly as he hit the floor. He left the room quickly, but he returned a moment later and moaned. In his mouth was a mouse, which he dropped, which scurried behind the wastebasket. The cat followed deliberately, but not rapidly, and then lay down, spreading himself out in front of the basket, his ears pricked forward. He was curious, just curious, about what was behind the wastebasket. For the next several hours he toyed with the mouse, played with it, occasionally taking time out for a catnap. I sat at my desk and wrote a little. I stared out at the growing cloud, leaning back in my chair. I flipped through books on nationalism in Central Europe, the effect of geography on political choice, and I tried to calculate in months how long it had been since I'd seen Alexander. For a long time during those first months and years after his birth, I knew exactly how many weeks it had been, and if the number didn't come to mind immediately when I stopped to think about it, I would panic. How could I lose track of that exact number? I felt I'd betrayed him, and I'd lost something, yet again lost something. After about seventy weeks I forced myself to stop keeping track. What good did it do? But months were easier—that just took a little counting, some easy multiplying. The gray cloud brightened around the edges. The orange cat moaned fondly at his mouse. Take the number of years, multiply by twelve. Add on a few months, let's see, four. One hundred and twelve. Abandoned for 112 miserable months.

The books and articles that well-meaning friends supply tell you all about the process of grief. Once in a while the books get something right, but more often they irritate or anger you. They tell you about anger and denial and depression; they say little about separation, and nothing at all about time. At least not the books I read. Time was the enemy and a wall, a solid stone wall between us, that kept growing larger and thicker as it gathered to it seconds and weeks and bricks and months and stones. Whole seasons pushed their way between my baby and me. I was frightened by the time interposing itself between my son's life and the moment in which I lived. Time made me furious, and I could do nothing but watch it grow, and for a long while that's all I did. In grief and fury I watched time grow. The time between us was as long as his life—thirteen days; then it was as long as my pregnancy. Could I recall his face any longer, or just my memory of his face? Experts of memory say you are just recalling your memories. More layers between us. The time between us was a year, then several years. I envied the women whose sons drowned at three, or committed suicide when they were about to turn seventeen. What a lot those women had to hold onto... But I never wanted to be a different mother. I just wanted my tiny baby. He was tiny, a baby you held carefully in hour hands. You couldn't cradle him, alive, in your arms. There was not enough there and there were too many wires ready to be confused or disconnected. He was tiny, but he wasn't, by any means, the tiniest in the RNICU. When my husband and I furtively returned to the nursery a month after our baby's death—a whole month between us, a time more than twice as long as his life—we realized that the baby who, weeks earlier, lay on the table next to Alexander's, a baby who had been much smaller and much sicker than Alexander, who had, sometimes, been covered with an aluminum space blanket to help keep him warm, was still alive, and nearly five weeks old. We found that the tiny, almost translucent Adam had grown and had graduated to the room across the hall. In that room, nurses and parents regularly sat in the rocking chairs, rocking the babies. Sometimes they even fed the babies bottles. Those babies were quite coordinated and mature—they could handle sucking and breathing and swallowing, all by themselves. When Alexander was in the RNICU, my husband had told me that tiny Adam's father would come, and he would cry as he sat beside the baby's warming table. My husband felt slightly guilty because our baby, who was several ounces beneath his birth weight of three pounds, one ounce, was so big and was doing so well. That tiny Adam, if he lived, would be nine years old now, older than my daughter and even taller. Now there were more than nine years between my son and me, 112 miserable months. Only occasionally now do Adam's parents consider those early months of fear sprinkled with small gleams of hope, the intense fear that, like grief, tightens all the muscles in your neck and back, makes your hands hurt, your throat ache.

The gray cloud covered all the sky; it no longer had bright edges and it was sinking onto the mountains. Minutes, or even an hour ago, I had closed my window whose glass preserved long dried raindrops and flecks of last summer's bugs, but I couldn't remember whether the cat was in or out, whether the cat was orange or gray. I glanced at the beds and cushions and chairs, which were empty.

I called from the window of my study, from the front door. The sounds were swallowed by the outside that was gray and still, waiting for the hiss of snow, waiting for the cry of a cat. I had to get the children, but I'd never left the house with the cat outside before. Always a first time. I backed out the car. If it started to snow, he could find shelter under the deck or in the entryway. And if the coyotes came close to the house? I turned on the car heater and was buffeted by gusts of cold air.

At his school, Benjamin greeted me, smiling broadly, hugging his bunny. He kissed me and touched my face. "It was fun, today. It was *fun*."

"I'm glad. Now we have to go get Mariana."

"I know. Mommy?"

"Yes?"

"I love you."

"I love you too. So much."

"Pick me up. Please, will you pick me up?"

The road from the preschool to the elementary school goes by several new houses; it goes by the old elementary school. It goes by the graveyard. I was in that graveyard only once, and it was before I had my own children. A three-year-old boy who'd drowned in a pond not fifty yards from his parents' house was buried in that graveyard. We'd searched all night for him, after he disappeared in the afternoon. All the family and all the neighbors and Rocky Mountain Rescue had searched. They discovered his small body at dawn, when they checked the pond for the third or fourth time. The little boy died in the early summer, but the day of his funeral was cold and raw with little sunshine and a considerable wind. The grass was green in the graveyard on the hillside above the town. In graveyards they lower children and they lower dead babies who have been gently wrapped and placed in small coffins that are not small enough. They lower the coffins carefully into the holes, and the mourners angrily kick in the dirt. Birds complain in the spruce trees an arthritic doctor planted nearly a hundred years earlier. No one notices the birds. A semi-trailer moving uphill on the highway lets loose a cloud of gray exhaust. Everyone is offended. They keep on lowering bodies into the small, neatly cut graves. Soon the cemetery will be quite full.

It was snowing harder as we drove past the cemetery. Snow blew in the car as Mariana climbed in, but by the time we got home, the snow had ceased, and there was blue sky in the west. I was disappointed. I'd been expecting a major spring storm for weeks, for more than a month. This was not to be it. No cat darted out from under the deck as I pulled into the carport. By now the cat should want to come in. He could not tolerate the snow.

Benjamin watched me as I pulled off his boots. He was smiling, his face was slightly pink.

"Mommy?"

"Yes?"

"I love you."

"I love you too." I put the boots in the closet.

He says "I love you" because he's forgotten what he planned to say, or because he expected something brilliant and important to leap to mind, and then he has to say something to fill in the blank. Still, after he speaks, he believes it—he has, recently, been falling in love with me. I know he's in love because of the way he looks at me when he hugs and kisses me. Delight and knowledge are in that look: I am his, he knows he is mine. He pulls back for a moment and touches my cheek. The love fills us up.

He didn't always have so much love for me. Me, he needed and took for granted; his father was the focus of his love and the center of his life. When Benjamin was nearly one, I underwent another abdominal surgery, and for him I became nearly useless as a parent; I couldn't lift him: that might rip out my stitches. So Benjamin crawled to the parent who would pick him up, who would carry him round and round the living room in the backpack to ready him for bed. He preferred his father for months, for years after that. And for months and years I was jealous. Now, it wasn't that he preferred me, but he had rediscovered me. That was a wonder to me.

And I wanted Alexander to love me like that.

This was a new loss. Surprise, surprise. And I'd assumed by now that I'd uncovered every one. The losses used to hit you over the head daily, hourly. That afternoon I nearly welcomed the devastation. It was, after all, a familiar feeling.

The children were running through the house in their socks, looking for the orange cat, discarding socks and coats and sweaters. The mouse appeared first. "What's this?" Mariana cried, holding a curled body between her thumb and finger. She'd found it in the toe of her slipper. Benjamin appeared holding the cat who, in his arms, was limp, passive, and nearly half the size of my son.

"Good," I said, and hugged my son and the cat. The cat growled. "Where did you find him?"

"He was in the closet. He wasn't asleep."

"You heard me call," I said to the cat, and asked the children to hang up their coats.

I put on the teakettle and built a fire. The cat crouched next to the living room stove, watching me, waiting for the spread of heat.

How much I loved Alexander. I *was* allowed that much. Some mothers of preemies, I've read, are frightened, even estranged by the web of connections between the small, strange creature and so many machines. Not me. I ignored those wires and tubes. I remember thinking, I ought to learn what all the machines are for, but I can't do it now. There wasn't time. I had to take in his fingernails, his cheek. Three days after his birth I was overawed by the beauty of his tiny mouth. I hadn't especially noticed it before. Not until I was back in my room did I realize that I'd not previously paid attention to his mouth because a large, plastic, ridged ventilator tube had, up until that morning, been shoved through his mouth and stuck in his throat. That morning, three days after his birth, he'd been extubated, and allowed to breathe on his own.

I was allowed to love Alexander. This was not allowed: for him to love me, to know that he loved me. For me to know he knew he loved me.

Does it matter? I just want to see him eat breakfast, to poke at his oatmeal, put his spoon down and say, "I'm done."

At the kitchen table Benjamin squawked; then he growled, loudly. He was drawing, at least he was trying to draw, a chimney on a house, and the orange cat, sitting on the table just above his paper, was moving his tail slowly back and forth over the paper. Benjamin made various noises at the cat who ignored him, noises that increased in volume and intensity. He poked at the cat with his pencil.

"Careful," I warned and swept up the cat, removing him to the counter beside his food dish.

In the dim, quiet room where Benjamin was born, the midwife handed him to me immediately after birth, and I felt triumph and panic. *So this is my new son*, and, *How do you take care of someone so tiny?* Although at six pounds, thirteen ounces, he was well over twice Alexander's weight, although I knew we had, more or less successfully, cared for Mariana two and a half years earlier, I'd no idea how we'd managed. This baby was so little and slippery, so much inside of his own world which did not include air and other people. The mingled feelings of admiration and fear continued through Benjamin's early months. And I was never separated from him for more than a couple of hours until I underwent surgery when he was eleven months old. He slept, when he slept, in the cradle by our bed. I nursed him when he woke, which was often, and held him anxiously as he drifted back into sleep. His breathing was labored, there was yellow matter on his eyes, his fever was up, was it? I was frightened, overly protective, as I'd expected to be with Mariana, but we were fortunate with Mariana: she was healthy, she was a girl. But this small son, who looked a little like Alexander, who, like Alexander, like probably at least fifty percent of normal, healthy babies, adjusted with some reluctance to the world of air and people, returned me to the world of fear and sick babies. When I left him, for an hour or two in order to exercise, or to do some quick shopping, I only left him in the care of my husband, or, occasionally, my mother. Benjamin had fevers, he caught colds; after a night of high fever when he was two months old, he turned a dusky green and, confirming my fears, was rushed in an ambulance to the hospital where, on oxygen and antibiotics, he began to recover, immediately. The next winter, when

I had to be hospitalized, I was afraid to leave him, although by then he was fat and thriving. He did, still, manage to get sick every week or two. That fall Mariana had started preschool, and it seemed that she brought all the new germs home to her brother. Mariana remained healthy; Benjamin got sick. And he recovered.

Two days, three days before I was to fly to Houston for my surgery, I was always watching Benjamin, dreading our separation. I was afraid Benjamin would get sick while I was gone, and I was certain he would forget me. Before I left, he'd be playing happily in the living room with his father and sister until I walked by or until he saw me in the kitchen; then he'd reach out his arms and cry. It was all I needed, a week before I left, to hear my mother-in-law's cheerful question on the phone: "And how will you feel when you come back, and your baby doesn't know you?"

At the kitchen table Benjamin scowled at his chimney. "It's poopy," he said.

"It looks fine to me." The left side was not perfectly symmetrical with the right, but the two sides looked good together. The chimney had a jaunty look. "You make good chimneys." I had no idea what we could have for supper—we'd had spaghetti the night before.

"You never help me," Benjamin crumbled the paper and threw it on the floor.

"Come on, Benjamin," I retrieved the paper and smoothed it out. "Your chimney is fine. I think your house just might like a few windows."

"That paper is all wrinkly! I can't draw on it!"

Mariana, who had just bounced into the room, leaned over the table. "Your chimney's crooked," she said. Benjamin jumped from his chair, ready to attack her. I wondered how I was going to fix supper. And why did we have to eat every single night?

Throughout the evening the children were wild. Benjamin rolled a ball across the living room. Mariana kicked it under the couch. He howled. Mariana picked up his bunny from the chair, tossed it into the air so that it landed back in the chair. "Put it back the way it was!" Benjamin cried. I looked at the clock and calculated the number of minutes until bedtime. A moment later I looked again. The day after I'd returned from the hospital, nearly three and a half years earlier, I'd been so thrilled to see the children. My husband and I had returned at night, and the next morning Mariana came and climbed into our bed. We held each other—we had to make up for so much time. In the next few weeks, we had to hold each other and hold on. I'd thought, before I left, that I'd be all right, leaving Mariana—we could talk on the phone, after all. But I never anticipated how much I'd miss her physically—I never thought of how much I needed to hold her every day. The reunion with Benjamin, of course, was different. He was nearly one, and when my husband brought him into our bed that first morning, the baby gave me a quizzical look, half smiling. *Do I know you?* he was thinking. He wasn't afraid of me. He was indifferent. We had a good day. I was shaky, but happy, and by six o'clock, at the dinner table, I was thinking, I love them, I'm so glad to see them, but can't the children go to bed now?

Benjamin did not resist going to school Wednesday morning. I hoped we had made some sort of breakthrough. More likely, it was just an easy day. He objected once, Tuesday night, when he was talking to his father. "I don't want to go to school tomorrow. I hate school." In the morning he said, "I don't want oatmeal. I hate oatmeal." Then he ate a few bites. I braced myself when I asked him what sort of sandwich he wanted for lunch ("I don't want any sandwich! I don't want to go to school!"), and he answered, "Turkey."

"Turkey or egg salad?"

"Turkey and egg salad."

The sky was low and gray, the air was damp when I drove the children to school, but it was not yet snowing. At the pre-school, after I helped Benjamin from the car, I unfastened his car seat and carried it to the school van where I strapped it in. There was a field trip scheduled to the Garfield County Library, and I hoped the snow would hold off until the van returned from the library. I'd forgotten about the field trip when I'd suggested to Benjamin's teacher that I stay at school for a while on Wednesday. Now, they'd be bustling around inside, preparing. I'd be in the way, and, when the van left, my separation from Benjamin would be abrupt after all. I decided that today, at any rate, I'd better leave the school as usual. I placed the car seat in the school van, and I tried to pull the seat belt tight through its openings, but you could never get the belt tight enough. I thought I should forget about the car seat. Benjamin was four, so the car seat was no longer required by law: perhaps he would be safer without it. How can you decide? I left the car seat in the van, secured as well as I could manage, and, trying to shake off an image of the van sliding off a snow-covered road and tumbling down a ravine, the car seat sliding from side to side on the seat, its straps pressing hard against my son's neck, I walked across the playground with Benjamin, who said, "After you go, I will be sad. I will cry."

"You're going to have a good time. You're going to the library."

Inside we put Benjamin's lunch box in his cubby, and we put his bunny in with his pillow and blanket on the blanket shelf. "You have to give me lots of hugs and kisses," Benjamin said. He got a puzzle from the shelf and sat down with it. I hugged him. He said calmly, "I'll cry after you go. I'll be sad."

"No," I lied. "You'll be fine." What do I know? After I go, I'll be gone. "I love you." I kissed him again and walked away. Benjamin got up from his chair as I hurried out the door.

The road up to our house was newly covered with snow when I drove home. On the lower part of the road, I passed a neighbor leaving for work, and farther up, observing her tire tracks, I wondered vaguely about her state of mind. Did she assume every morning that she owned the road, or was she simply late today? The tracks, around the corner, were on my side of the road. For long stretches they held the center of the road. Most days this neighbor could escape the subdivision without subjecting herself to this analysis. Most days, by the time I reached the next corner, I'd have forgotten I ever passed her. This morning there was a preschool van lumbering south on the Peak to Peak Highway, and dozens of cars coming toward it, blindly, recklessly, around corners on the wrong side of the road.

By the time I was working at my desk, it had been snowing lightly for some time; occasionally the snow would thicken. This late winter weather threatened at times to turn into a great spring storm, appeared at times ready to break apart to clearing skies, even sunshine. Was this rain or snow in front of the trees? A small flock of juncos flew toward the limber pine. At one moment, each bird landed on a different branch, so there was no longer a flock. Just a tree, slightly decorated, with a little less snow than before.

It was snowing the day Alexander died. "His first snow," my husband said.

And he'll never see snow.

No one said that. Did we think it then, or later?

He was beautiful after he died. I wouldn't say he was at peace. His expression was more intent than that. He wasn't disengaged. Just resting. "We'll clean him up," the nurse said, "then bring him to you in the parents' room, so you can hold him." I was surprised. I had no idea that attitudes towards grief could be humane. I came from a world that masked grief, that refused to acknowledge death. "We've found it helps to say good-bye," the nurse said. She was sad, she was gentle. How often did she, working in the intensive care unit of Children's Hospital, have to hand dead babies to their parents? I realized I was looking forward to holding him. I had, after all, only held him once before.

With a Polaroid camera, the nurse took a couple of pictures of this beautiful baby. Nurses keep Polaroids handy. At the hospital across the street, a nurse in the RNICU had taken Alexander's picture soon after he was born, as had a different nurse when I held him for the first time, and when my husband had held him. The early images bore some slight resemblance to the baby; these final pictures were ghastly: in the photograph he was a dark orange color, his eyes stuck out. He seemed to be in agony or constipated. Even so, afterwards, I cherished the ghastly pictures along with the half-dozen sedate ones, and when I thrust the pictures in front of my sisters weeks later, months later, they gamely attempted not to recoil. "It doesn't look like him, he was really beautiful," I insisted. My sisters said nothing; what could they say? I wanted them to appreciate the pictures, if not the baby, although for a time I'd been afraid to look at the pictures, the good ones and the bad ones, at all. I was afraid those images would supersede my memories of the living baby.

The cat came up to my chair to stretch. He reached up with his front paws, snagging the chair, snagging my mid-section. "Hey!" I cried. He jumped away and crouched down. After that he wouldn't come near me for what seemed like hours. "You started it," I said. Not that he listened, not that he cared.

I held my dead baby for hours in the parents' room, which had a blue couch, flowered wallpaper, and no windows. He had been ill for just over twenty-four hours. The morning before, blood in the stool, nurses and residents hovering over his table, life supports reattached—ventilator and IVs. In the afternoon, transported across the street for surgery at Children's. The limp body after surgery. The limp body in the morning when the anesthesia had long worn off. The sober residents looking down at the limp body: *Sometimes these little guys surprise you. Sometimes they hang on for hours, even days.* We watched the chest move up and down: the ventilator was doing its job. They sent us away while they performed some procedure, sent us to the room with flowered wallpaper and no windows, and came in a few minutes later to say he was gone. Why did they send us away? A little while later we were back in the room with the small bundle of blankets, no wires attached. I was generous at times and relinquished the baby for short periods to my husband, who sobbed. His grief frightened me. It was all my fault, after all. I'd upended my husband's life and heaped this grief on him because I wanted a baby, because I had to have a baby. When my husband handed me the baby again, I unwrapped the blankets and examined the tiny body. He was mine. In the RNICU where the nurses held sway, making all the decisions, where I was the ignorant bystander, too often in the way, I could never be sure that Alexander was truly my baby. Now, on my lap, this was my baby; he had tiny nipples. They were just dots and I'd never seen them before. While he was alive those dots had been covered by small patches attaching monitors to his thin chest. It was all right, now, as long as they didn't take him away. He had a chest I could put my hands around. I could hold my son, my little one.

Gusts of snow moved before the tree from left to right, pushed by the wind that now came from the east, an upslope. Birds traded branches; they made a lot of noise, chattering, even singing, defying the snow. I was quite alone—my husband at work, my children at school.

How can they go on without me? It's incomprehensible that they can be in worlds I don't experience. Mariana, holding herself quiet in her chair, hoping, hoping—at this moment nothing else in the world really matters to her—praying the teacher will choose her table next to line up for PE. Benjamin, sitting on the library floor, listening to a story. He can't see the pictures very well, but at school he doesn't complain. Or perhaps he's not at school, but in the back of the dirty white van as it slides around corners on its way home from the library. The van has snow tires of course, but it doesn't have four-wheel drive, and the snow's coming down much harder than before. It's no use calling the school—what could they do besides lie and reassure. News of an accident, if there's an accident, will take some time to reach them.

I had no idea what was going on. How could I not know?

In the parents' room at Children's, in the room with flowered wallpaper and the blue couch, we held the baby and talked and cried. I don't know if I cried. The doctors came in and out, murmuring. The chaplain stood awkwardly in the door. We looked at him blankly. "If there's anything I could do to help," he said.

The head doctor of the RNICU, who was on duty at Children's that day, came in. He said, "You can't hold him forever, you know."

Thank you very much.

And I did plan on holding him forever. After all they wouldn't dare to wrest him away from me. I stroked the perfect hand, but the small body had less presence. Even as I held his body, my baby was farther and farther away.

After a while I did let them take away the small bundle that was my baby's body; I must have let them take it away because I don't have it any longer. After a while we were standing in the nurses' kitchen supply room, and I was dizzy. This was the rest of my life, and, along with the metal cupboards and the uncharacteristically idle nurses, the rest of my life was the indifferent background of a movie someone had decided not to shoot. The chaplain, as always, stood in the doorway. He said, "Please let me know if there's anything I can do to help."

"Well," my husband said, "maybe you can get her a wheelchair. She's not really strong enough to stand and walk just now."

Something moved in the large ponderosa outside. Clumps of snow fell, and the orange cat appeared on a branch high above the ground. I'd never seen him in a tree before, but without a thought he leapt to the branch above him, climbed higher, then turned and came back down around the trunk. He bounded through the snow to my window. His cries came through the glass and continued after I let him in. Angry and indignant, he stalked up and down my desk, leaving wet footprints on my paper, his tail brushing my face. The preschool van must be returning from the Garfield library. It might be back from the library, it might be in a ditch, better in a ditch than down a cliff. I gave up trying to write and went upstairs to feed the cat, to make a cup of tea. I gathered a load of laundry while I waited for the water to boil. It annoyed me that instead of working I was wasting my precious time alone, worrying about the children: there were only two hours left before it would be time to retrieve them. I could, while I drank my tea, at least try to penetrate the fat, dull volume on the Ottoman Empire. I glanced at the phone and turned away—it was good, wasn't it, that the phone did not ring, did not deliver tales of bent guardrails and bruised flesh. As I sat on the couch with my tea and the Ottomans, who seeped decorously into the Balkans, the water poured into the washing machine. B flat above middle C. You can hear the drops. Once in a while, as I'm falling asleep, I try to figure out how many loads of laundry I've done in my life, or in a year. It's not a good time to do math in your head, while you're falling asleep. You forget whether you're calculating for life, or just a year. You fall asleep feeling uneasy, incompetent.

The washer's agitation began, a comforting sound, when you stop to listen to it, and even when you don't, and the Ottomans were surprisingly accommodating, no matter what you are led to believe during the Balkan disturbances of the present day.

At the crematorium they sweep the ashes from the furnace into a plastic bag. They roll down the top of the bag and place it in the bottom of a small box made of particleboard. Contact paper, simulating wood grain, covers the outside of the box. The plastic bag nestles in the bottom corner of the box. The rest of the box is filled with dark air.

My eyes were not open when a voice repeated a phrase in a foreign language, maybe German, maybe Turkish. The voice had come from the hallway, even though no one was in the hall. I thought I should write down the phrase, guess at the spelling, but I was afraid by the time I opened my eyes and picked up a pencil I'd forget the words, and when I'd opened my eyes and found a pencil, the words were gone. I located my coat and my car keys—it was time to pick up the children from school. Had the words been a warning? It was a good thing, at any rate, that the voice had waked me—already I was on the verge of being late, and the drive in this snow would take considerably longer than usual. The wipers smeared snow across the windshield. I tried to focus on the snow ahead of the car, but the flakes kept bringing my gaze back to the windshield, and when I forced it out again, the gaze tangled with the snowflakes. A man's voice uttered a German or Turkish phrase. I braked gently; the car swerved and my stomach tightened.

We placed the box on a shelf in the spare bedroom closet. I didn't forget it was there; still, I was startled when I opened the closet door and saw it. A couple of weeks later, when we flew west, we carried the box aboard the plane in a daypack. It fit awkwardly in the pack, one corner pressing hard against the fabric.

I was late retrieving Mariana at the elementary school. Usually I try to arrive early to intercept her as she comes out the door, in case she has forgotten I'm picking her up and heads for the bus. She was not waiting at the door; she was not on the bus. I found her finally, waiting inside of the door, out of the snow and wind. She was annoyed; we were both relieved. I told her to hurry. "We have to get Benjamin, he'll be wondering where we are."

The van was parked next to the preschool in its usual place, with no new dents. Snow had drifted up against the tires. Mariana and I brought snow in with us onto the preschool floor where the children in their socks drifted across the room, carrying pillows and blankets to the hall shelves.

Benjamin, clutching his bunny, was still sleepy. I wondered if he had heard a voice in the other room before he awoke. Quite possibly he had: during naptime the teachers, cutting out flower templates from tag board, had been talking to each other, but not, most likely, in Turkish. I asked Kathie about the trip to the library as I helped Benjamin with his boots and coat.

"Oh, we didn't go. We never take a chance, if the weather looks at all bad."

I drove home slowly in the snow. The children squabbled in the back of the car.

My husband and I carried the particleboard box into the national forest. We opened it on top of a small hill. An out-cropping of rock marked the hill, which was out of sight of the dirt road, but within an easy walk from it. A dirty, thick plastic bag rested in the bottom of the box. It was just a dirty bag. In the bag was only a small amount of ash. A little bit of ash, blowing away in the wind. Bits of bone. We were left with the empty bag, which we folded and hid under a rock. We didn't consider that littering. Later, we didn't know what to do with the box, so we burned it in the fireplace, contact paper and all.

In the evening Benjamin called from the children's bedroom. I'd put the children to bed more than half an hour before, and Mariana was on her side, asleep.

"I'm scared to go to sleep," Benjamin said.

I kissed him. Was he warm? He seemed warm. I could go kiss Mariana to compare the body temperature. "It will be all right," I said.

"If you wake up when you're halfway through a dream, will you dream the rest of the dream when you go back to sleep?"

"Oh, no. I wouldn't worry about that. Did you wake up part-way through a dream last night?"

"No. It was a dream I had at my nap. When I was at school. It was a bad dream."

"Do you want to tell me about it?"

"No. I don't want to say it. If I go to sleep, will I dream the rest of the dream?"

"I'm sure you won't. I'll sit with you a few minutes and rub your back. I bet you won't dream anything when you go to sleep."

"Daddy has nipples," he said as I rubbed his back.

"So do you."

But why, he wanted to know, do boys have nipples, when they don't make milk for babies.

"Well, because . . ." I thought of vestigial organs, but not the right answer. I'm not very good, anymore, at answering his questions. The orange cat came in and jumped onto the end of his bed. What if I'd never met my husband, never had children, never lost children? What if I'd lived my life alone with this orange cat?

Benjamin sat up to pat the cat. I told Benjamin I didn't know why he had nipples, but he shouldn't worry about it now. Someday he could learn why—he'd learn it in a book or at school.

"Do I go to school tomorrow?"

"Not tomorrow, you went today."

"After tomorrow, do I go?"

"You'll go on Friday."

"No! I hate school!"

"Oh, Benjamin. Always, when I pick you up at school, you say you had a good time. Really, you like school. Besides, you have to go to school so you can learn how to answer all the questions you ask. They're getting to be too hard for me. Anyway, tomorrow you don't have to go."

He grabbed his bunny and turned on his side. The windows rattled—the wind was coming up again. I went to sit on the edge of Mariana's bed since Benjamin wouldn't let himself sleep while I sat beside him, and as I moved, the cat crept up to Benjamin's pillow, next to his head. I touched Mariana's back. Always in motion during the day, she was now so absolutely still. That amazed me. When she was an infant, when, finally she fell asleep, I would stare at her body in disbelief. Sleep is nearly as incomprehensible as death. Where does she go? Is it possible I can move and breathe without every second attending to her, worrying about her, watching out for her?

In sleep, there is separation, as well.

I looked at Benjamin who was staring at me.

"You're supposed to be asleep."

"No. If I go to sleep, I'll dream the rest of that bad dream."

NEXT STOP

Although Emily had always preferred walking to riding the bus, in September she found she frequently took the bus to and from work. It was because she was often tired in the fall; it was because she now lived farther from the center of the city. On the bus she sat like the other riders with her hands on the railing before her, or with her hands on her lap. Like the other riders, since the bell on the bus didn't work, she said, "Next stop, please," when she wanted to get off.

Emily was pleased that she could ride calmly on the bus since she'd spent years avoiding buses. Buses were among the things that had frightened her as a child. Other things that frightened her were flies in the corner of the bathroom, colored magazine pictures with camels' feet cut off by the bottom of the page, and her brothers' anonymous voices on the other end of the phone. As Emily grew up, she'd learned to open the window wide to let out the flies, to turn the magazine pages quickly, and to distinguish between the sounds of her brothers' voices, but for years she remained uneasy around buses.

As she rode, Emily tightened the pressure on her knuckles, looked at the smudges on the window, and watched the brick schoolhouses that passed one after another on Union Avenue and River Street. Some of the schools were made of blond brick, some were made of red brick, but all of them had double doors that opened into the gymnasiums, scuff marks on the cafeteria linoleum, half-circles painted on the playground. All of them had empty desks. Some of the schools had orange and yellow construction paper leaves taped to the windows. Some had no windows. Emily knew that even in the schools with no windows, kindergartners and first graders spent hours in the afternoon tracing the shapes of maple leaves on different colored construction paper. She knew the desks were empty because in the morning when she rode to work, the children were still at home puncturing the yolks of their fried eggs with forks, or they were on their way to school, kicking round stones away from younger neighbor children who wanted to kick the same stones. In the late afternoon when Emily rode home, she knew the children were all hanging from the monkey bars in the park or rolling footballs under the wheels of parked cars while they thought up elaborate excuses to avoid the next day's piano lessons.

Even if she did have to ride the Number Three bus all the way to the city's Riverside section, even if she did have to ride by so many brick schoolhouses, Emily was glad that she had decided, after all, to take the upstairs room in the green-shingled house. She was glad because she liked the handsome staircase in the center of the house, and because she liked the woman with gray streaks in her hair who had let her the room.

In August Emily had walked up and down the same block on Russell Street several times a day. She had admired the oddly shaped shingles on the pale green house. In August Emily craned her neck to see the orange room-for-rent sign in the third story window, and she considered what the view from the window would be. On a Thursday when Emily finally climbed the long stairs and knocked, the woman with gray streaks in her hair showed Emily into the kitchen beside the stairs. She told Emily her name was Dorinda, and she said the room was already rented.

Emily didn't believe her. She said, "That's probably just as well. I'd have to ride the bus all the way out here every day from work; then I'd have to ride it back the next morning. And I'm not at all fond of riding buses."

"I'll take your number if you like," Dorinda said, "I'm always glad to pin people's numbers on my bulletin board."

After Emily moved into the upstairs front room of the green house, Dorinda told her it would take her a while to get used to the stairs. Emily said she didn't mind—the stairs pleased her; she considered herself fortunate to live in a house bisected by stairs. After Emily moved, in the early fall, Emily and Dorinda spent hours in evenings, and some minutes in the dark early mornings waiting for the kettle to heat and making up stories about their pasts.

"When I was little, I'd be alarmed if I couldn't tell who was talking to me on the phone," Emily said as her coffee cooled. "I'd get upset when pictures of animals were carelessly cropped. I was even wary around buses, but I don't let them bother me now."

"I'd stay out late on weeknights," Dorinda responded. "Just before dawn I'd climb back in—through the back window."

While Dorinda and Emily talked, they often heard footsteps going up and down on the outside steps. Emily would be relieved when the sounds stopped and no one knocked on their door. To conceal her relief, Emily continued with the stories. She had left several brothers with familiar names; she rarely revealed their names. Dorinda had moved away from a large family in Florida and had crashed a green convertible. For a while now she'd lived in the pale green house on Russell Street. Before that she had had a habit of moving, and when she moved she left things behind—a husband or two, and four children, Emily thought, maybe five.

"Will you stay here for a while, do you think?" Emily asked.

"Oh, I think so. But I always think so. I moved in last fall, if I remember. Pretty good for me. After a while, you know, you start imagining things: it's as if you're being followed. You're just imagining it, you know, but it's hard, after all, to keep your imagination under control."

Emily asked about her children. It was difficult to ask, but the part about leaving them, she didn't understand.

"I couldn't believe it, that I was pregnant," said Dorinda. "The first time, of course, I was very young. You are, aren't you, very young?"

Emily shrugged. Not so very.

"When I was pregnant I thought, how could this be happening to me?" said Dorinda. "You know. How could it be? Now, in some ways it's the same. And of course they are better off, those children, they are much better off with their fathers. Perhaps that is hard to understand."

Emily thought she should say something. She should say she understood, she would try to understand. She listened to footsteps moving down the steps. That person, she thought, must walk with a limp.

In October there were more people on the bus than in September. Emily thought that perhaps more people had recently moved to the edge of town, or perhaps more people were pregnant. She had noticed recently a large number of pregnant women standing in line at the checkout counter of the supermarket, leaning against their metal baskets, lifting, one at a time, their feet because all of their shoes had recently grown too tight. She had noticed a large number of pregnant women waiting impatiently at the bus stop, and, as well, sitting placidly on the green seats inside the bus, staring at the schoolhouses that paraded by on the street. Some of the women wore voluminous pink maternity blouses with smocked yokes and cuffs. Some wore faded blue work shirts that must have belonged to their husbands or older brothers.

One evening in October a woman with a smocked pink maternity blouse moved carefully down the bus aisle. Emily expected the woman to take the empty seat beside her; instead, the woman sat behind her and looked out the window. At the next stop a young man with a blue tie, an umbrella, and a fading tan sat in the seat beside Emily. Emily avoided looking at the young man, and she wondered if the woman behind her had noticed the uncommon number of schools along the route.

The man beside Emily placed his umbrella in the aisle and cleared his throat. Emily looked out the window because she couldn't be bothered to talk at this time and because the man reminded her slightly of Nathan who used to ride buses with her in the spring.

She'd rather not think about Nathan; there wasn't, after all, a whole lot to think about. She saw, going by, two children with their shoelaces untied, picking dried leaves off the sidewalk, crumbling the leaves in their hands, filling their pockets with the dry crumbs. She thought it odd that the man next to her carried an umbrella since it had not rained in weeks; now, it was more likely to snow than rain.

The woman behind Emily on the bus said, "Next stop, please," and when the woman walked up the aisle, she held on to the seats on both sides of her. It occurred to Emily that in a month or two she would need to go after work to the Grand Worth Department Store to buy a pink smocked top.

When Emily said, "Next stop, please," and stood in the aisle, she hoped the man beside her wouldn't notice where she got off the bus. She didn't want him to follow her; she didn't need any more men running into her at bus stops or following her home. She enjoyed living with just Dorinda at the top of the stairs. Neither of them needed extra men around denting cushions on the couch, staring out the window, lighting cigarettes with the stove burner. She certainly didn't miss Nathan, the man she rode buses with last spring. Or, at least, she missed him only occasionally. Sometimes in the mornings, after breakfast; sometimes in the evenings, when she stood by the window. Nathan hadn't known she was pregnant when he left her late in the summer, and since she found it difficult to remember the days and their events in the proper order, she was never certain which, of the times that he left her, was the time he never returned again. It was possible that Emily didn't know she was pregnant when Nathan left her in the summer.

As the bus slowed, approaching Russell Street, Emily grasped a seat back to help her maintain her balance. As she walked toward the door at the rear of the bus, she occasionally placed a hand on a seat back on either side of the aisle.

Sometimes, that fall, Emily walked home, but her shoes were growing tight. She decided she got enough exercise just climbing the stairs to the third story of the house, and so, more and more often, she rode the bus. By late October it was dark outside, and young boys on her bus returning home from football practice made faces at the windows of the bus. Not long before Halloween, at the railway bridge, the young man with a blue tie got on and sat beside her. He carried an umbrella even though it was not raining, and he held it between his knees. The man with the tie was not the only man on the bus carrying an umbrella.

While Emily looked straight ahead, or at the schoolhouses outside the window, she wondered if he intended to speak.

"You missed your stop," he said finally.

"It doesn't much matter where I get off. Walking's not a problem."

The man said, "Next stop, please," and he stood up as the bus slowed. He said, "I thought I'd run into you again before this, but you aren't always on the bus."

"Sometimes I walk. It's not a problem."

"It's a long walk, when you're pregnant." He stepped into the aisle.

Emily said, "Don't forget your umbrella."

The next time the man sat beside Emily on the bus he offered her a peanut and told her his name was Lucas. He was wearing the same blue tie he had worn the week before. Emily was wearing a pink blouse with a smocked yoke.

"I've never seen so many men on the bus at once," Emily said. "Do you think it has something to do with the weather?"

"Could be."

"They come from all over the country, I think, and when they board the city buses, they sit across the aisle and in front of me and beside me. They are surveying the sidewalks, the schools, and the department stores. Most likely, they're making plans. They get off the bus at Fern Street and Chase Avenue, and they walk, tapping their umbrellas in front of Cherry Dale Elementary, and in front of the Grand Worth Store; then they board the cross-town bus and ride. They get off in front of the First Harvest Bank, I expect, and walk up and down on the sidewalks, tapping back and forth by South Ridge Junior High."

As the brick schoolhouses slid behind them, Emily noticed that most of the pregnant women on the bus wore plastic barrettes in their hair. Some of the women wore overcoats on top of their pink smocked blouses. Lucas offered Emily another peanut and said he'd been pursuing his missing sister for fifteen years. He had come close to finding her outside of Nashville, on a train north of Poughkeepsie, in a motel off the Pennsylvania Turnpike. He said that when her children came to stay with him, it was difficult, in the beginning, for him to become accustomed to the ways they resembled her. "But then it was difficult to get used to having children around at all. That's something you'll discover pretty soon." Lucas was staring at the pink gathered fabric beneath the smocking of her blouse.

"Unless, of course," he looked up suddenly, "unless you have other children."

Emily shook her head. She told him she had a roommate, and her roommate had had children, but they didn't live with her. "It is strange though," Emily said. "Once I never noticed children at all, but lately they've been surrounding me. Yesterday, the whole length of Grant Street, there was a yellow school bus beside us. The children on the city bus waved and cheered and pressed their noses and tongues against the window, but the children on the school bus pretended they never noticed. They stared straight ahead at the backs of the seats in front of them. Then the school bus went through a puddle at the corner of Grant and Josephine, and soon it was dark, so I couldn't tell what happened afterwards."

"It does get dark early now," Lucas said. "You'll want to be sure you don't miss your stop again; you wouldn't want to walk back to your house alone." He could accompany her; he would like to, but he had to get on home. There were the animals, and he had to be ready in case, just in case . . .

Lucas frequently sat beside Emily in the late fall when they rode home in the evening. Because it was dark outside, they could not easily make out the schools the bus passed, but since the bus lights were on, they could see each other, and they could see the other passengers on the bus, the umbrellas, the jackets buttoned tightly over blouses, the jackets not buttoned at all. Sometimes he asked her questions about her roommate, but Emily's answers were vague. She didn't know if her roommate had a favorite restaurant; at home she ate mostly eggs. She had a job, sure. Probably she talked about her job, but it wasn't the sort of talk you'd pay a lot of attention to. Other times, he asked her questions about her brothers. Emily said while she had several strange brothers with common names, not one of her brothers actually knew she was going to have a baby. "All the same," she said, "in the early morning when the city bus stops at a yellow light, and when, at that light, a huge silver and blue interstate bus stops and everyone inside looks directly at me, I'm certain that all the members of my family have boarded large buses, two steps at a time, and I'm certain that, except for my youngest brother Edward, who, by mistake has climbed on a yellow bus which follows its own circuitous route not to my front yard, but to the parking lot of a blond brick school, my other brothers on their Greyhounds, Trailblazers, and Bonanzas are coming to me, to this city to give my baby their names."

"I've heard that's the hardest part about having a baby, trying to decide on a name."

Emily sighed. She asked Lucas for ideas. He could tell her the names in his family.

There was Cristobel who was younger, there was Percival who was older, and his other sister who was older still; she was the one who had left home when he was still quite young. He asked the names of her brothers, and smiled when she said Edward, John, and George. He wanted to know if she kept in touch with her brothers. She said her brothers sent her cards at Christmas. She didn't bother to answer. They called occasionally to say that they meant to visit soon. They were just going to check out the bus schedules.

"I say, 'That would be nice.' Then we hang up."

All the windows of the schools the bus passed were lit up. Lucas said they were having parent-teacher conferences after school. He knew that because his nephew and nieces, when they visited, would sometimes attend school. He said they spent time with him in hopes that someday he would find their mother. He said once he liked to listen to opera in the evening, but he rarely did now.

One evening in March Emily left the bus without a thought at the corner of Russell Street and Parade. The bus left behind a fog of diesel, but Emily moved through it into the early evening on Russell Street where blots of snow crouched on the north sides of houses and on the grass where tree shadows lay in the mid-afternoon. As she walked, Emily maintained her balance successfully, although she was startled by faint pains in her lower abdomen, and by the shadows of cats in the corner of her eye. When she stood opposite the green house, she looked up at the third story window, but she could see no one looking out. She could only see dark glass and splotches of reflected sky.

As Emily crossed the empty street and damp lawn, she anticipated the pressure of the doorknob against the fingers of her glove; as she touched the doorknob she saw the stairs that rose for three flights and then ran into a window. By the time Emily had finished climbing the three flights of stairs, so much time had passed she thought it must be nearly morning, and time to walk down the stairs again. Since the apartment was empty and the bathroom was free, Emily took a bath, and she lay for a long time in the warm water. As she went back down the stairs in her bathrobe, Emily thought her pain might be contagious. She thought Dorinda might not want to be exposed. Dorinda might prefer that Emily take her pain elsewhere, away from the living room, but when she entered, she found that

that room, like the front bedroom, was dark. Later, as she moved about the dark living room waiting for her skin to dry, and waiting for her tea to brew, she imagined what she'd say when Dorinda returned. The ends of her hair were wet, and one hiss after another leapt up as the drops hit the radiator and her shoulders. While the air grew humid, Emily walked to the window and imagined Dorinda standing at the door of the house, deciding whether or not to enter. But indecision never occurred to Dorinda. She had no problem climbing on buses. Tea splashed against Emily's lower lip surprising her with pain. She could not, for a moment, remember why she was standing at the window staring down at the street, and she could not be sure why, since the tea had burned only her lip, there were pains in other parts of her body. With her hand she tried to locate a pain, but it disappeared, elusive. Emily looked down at the streetlamp and at the street. No one was looking up.

When she woke in the night Emily realized that she'd never heard Dorinda come in, and that the shape of the window was crooked against the wall. When she woke again with a tight throat, the window hung in a different place on the wall. She remembered hearing screams, although she remembered no dream.

When they told her in the hospital, she wondered if, maybe, it was just as well the baby had died. After all, it's a rough life, the life of a child: you spend so much time contained in blond brick buildings, squirming on hard plastic chairs. You peer through windows, all those dirty windows—school bus windows, school windows that open out, but not far enough: you can't push out your hand. You could, maybe, get something done with your life, but there's all that time you spend worrying about your mother, wondering if she's in the kitchen now or did she already go outside? Will she stick around? How long will your mother hang around?

Emily stared at the nightstand and nodded when the tall nurse told her. She knew the nurse was thinking that Emily nodded bravely. Emily nodded again, and then she started to scream. She wanted to know when. She cried, "When did the baby die?"

The nurse only said it was born dead; she wouldn't tell Emily when.

In the hospital they continued to call the baby it, although it had been born a boy. A dead boy. After a while Emily no longer screamed out loud, but she never knew how long she had carried him dead, on the buses, and up the stairs.

After she got out of the hospital, in the early spring, Emily rode the bus back and forth to work. To keep from thinking, she allowed the outlines of the buildings and the shapes of tree limbs to impress themselves below the clear space of her forehead, onto the smoothness of her cornea, but pictures of Dorinda's children would crowd out the buildings and tree branches and she would think of the ones abandoned in Texas and Nebraska. She thought of their bedrooms, and the small spaces between their toes. And then, except for the slight change of temperature on her cheek as shadow replaced sun, the buildings and trees moved by unnoticed.

Each day Emily was sure new buses came into the city, buses with silver and blue streaks, buses with windows framed in red, and, in the windows, eyes framed in blood. The buses were bringing in more men with umbrellas, bringing Dorinda's children, bringing her brothers from various corners of the country. The men with umbrellas had familiar names, like her brothers', or they had no names at all. She didn't know because they didn't tell her. Instead, they put their umbrellas beside them in the aisles when they sat down, and they picked the umbrellas up when they stood to get off the bus. No longer were there women with pink smocked blouses on the bus, or perhaps these women wore overcoats and kept their blouses covered up.

One morning Emily was frying eggs when Dorinda climbed the stairs and walked into the kitchen.

"I don't want to hear about your night," Emily said to the eggs. The butter coated the lace edges of the whites, turning them brown. Dorinda sat on the counter smoking and speaking. She turned on the radio, and Emily braced herself for the voice of a man selling bedroom furniture. She heard Schubert and she was grateful. As Dorinda smoked, some of her curls imitated the curve of the smoke, some imitated its color.

"When we went to Aram's rooms above the jewelry store," Dorinda said, "I thought of calling you, but I figured you'd be asleep."

"Besides, the phone is out of order."

"Yes, and Aram didn't even bother to turn on the light. You know, your eggs are growing hard."

Emily nodded. She looked at ashes piled in a very small mountain far below Dorinda's feet. She lifted the eggs with a fork—that was not easy—laid them on a cold plate, then, one at a time, picked up the tired eggs with thumb and finger and dropped them in the wastebasket.

A siren cried and Emily jumped.

"The siren's on the radio," Dorinda said.

"I understand." She carried the frying pan to the sink. It was an old sink, a deep one, and the water hit the center of the pan hard, splashing up the sides. "I don't understand about your brother and the children. I always used to see Lucas, but nowadays he's never on the bus."

"He's coming up with a plan." Dorinda was smiling. Her upper lip curled and revealed her teeth. "Lucas is only comfortable when he has a plan. Then he'll give me a call."

"And the phone doesn't work."

"Hmmm." Dorinda took a knife from the sink strainer and gestured toward Emily with the bone handle. "You think I should, after all this time, have something to do with those children. You're missing your baby, and you think you've got everything all figured out."

"I don't know about that." Now Emily was hungry and there were no more eggs.

Dorinda put out her cigarette.

One afternoon in late April, Emily waited for a bus that seemed to be a long time coming, and sparrows rustled among paper bags caught in the nearby bushes. This was not her usual bus, but she needed to get to the library. Maybe she would walk—it wasn't two miles. Perhaps it was two, perhaps more. Emily looked south toward Orange Street, as if she were watching the fat front of the bus lumbering north toward them, toward the Railway Bridge. You don't have to get on, she thought, but it was, perhaps, beginning to rain. Quiet people stood, waiting in the cold, in the rain. The young woman with two shopping bags and one child. The man with no shopping bags and no children whose briefcase stood between his shoes. The two blonde teenage girls who chewed gum and exchanged glances. Emily could not believe all of the people were waiting for the bus with absolute assurance. One of them must be thinking—when the bus came, he'd bolt.

When she was on the bus Emily looked away from the four chewed fingers on the seat rail in front of her and toward the window. They passed a red brick elementary school on Water Street with empty seesaws in the playground, a gray brick department store on Saratoga Avenue, a house with large windows, a woman combing her hair, a woman with her throat cut. There were smudges on the window of the bus. There was an empty seat beside her, and Emily was afraid men with umbrellas would sit and tell her stories she had heard before. For a while no one sat beside her, although a few men with umbrellas were actually on the bus. Also, many more were on the sidewalk. Emily was certain that the city was being besieged. Small pellets of rain disturbed the patterns on the bus windows, and men with umbrellas said, "Next stop, please," got off the bus, walked rapidly down the sidewalks, and, in unison, tapped their umbrella points on the sidewalk. She knew they were deciding on the moment they would stop tapping the sidewalk and would start knocking against the windows of the department stores. She knew, when she wasn't looking, the men opened and closed their umbrellas, arranging blots of color against the brick-gray background, generating small gusts of wind.

Lucas was waiting at a stop north of Wildwood Park. As he approached her, down the aisle, he appeared surprised to see her.

"You've lost weight," he said.

Emily said she was riding to the South Branch Library in search of a book on Peruvian artifacts. They passed a brick school with small-pane windows, a cemetery without any grass. South of Bryant Avenue, snow was falling, although it was late April.

Lucas remarked on the snow, saying he'd arrived last fall in a snowstorm, and when, three weeks ago, his niece, Alexandra arrived, it was snowing as well.

"Then, of course, it was just March. It's supposed to snow in March."

"I expect Dorinda told you Alexandra was here. She's spoken with her on the phone, more than once. I think Dorinda was quite happy to hear from her. Don't you? Quite soon, we think, she'll be ready for a meeting."

There was an explosion as the bus passed Centennial High School. The bus windows rattled.

"It's those men, the ones with the umbrellas you know," Emily was nodding. "They've finally begun their demolition. What were you saying about your niece?"

"She's in touch with the others. They want to come out. We're trying to ease Dorinda into the idea. She'll get to know the children when they visit, and if things go well, and I think they should, we'll all go back to Texas together. Maybe in the summer, in the early summer, before it gets too hot."

"When was the last time you spoke to Dorinda?"

"A few days, not long ago. And I know Alexandra's been in touch."

"But she's gone, you know. Last week. She took off and I'm stuck with the rent. It's a lot more than I can afford. On top of everything else, I need to advertise for a roommate.

The woman across the aisle said, "Next stop, please," and a dark plume of smoke rose from the roof of the K-Mart building. Lucas's head twisted to follow the gaze of the people on the sidewalk and the other people on the bus.

"What do you know," Emily remarked, and the bus stopped in the middle of Grant Street. No one got off.

"You must have a forwarding address. You can give it to me."

Emily nodded. "I'll think about it," she said, "but now I've got to go to the library before they blow up the books on Peruvian artifacts."

"I wouldn't worry about it yet," Lucas said. "They seem to be concentrating on schools and department stores."

At the end of the month Emily purchased an umbrella. She had never owned one before. She set the umbrella carefully behind the rocking chair in her room. She was afraid, if she carried it, she would leave it on the bus.

Stranger

Diana did not speak until she finished her orange juice. She ran her finger around the inside edge of the glass and licked it. "My sister left," Diana said, "and when she did, she left her hands behind. I hid them in the fruit bowl beneath the oranges. I was ready to leave as well, but there was no one then to leave with me."

The sunlight hit the hood of Timothy's pickup and came through the diner window to land beside his napkin.

"I didn't know you had a sister," he said.

"Why should you know? Two days ago you were a stranger in Salina, walking across the room, a little slower than the rest, a little darker than the rest."

Diana could not see his face well now because it was in shadow before the bright window. She found it difficult to look at his face anyway, so she looked at his hands.

"Is your tea sweet enough?" he asked.

She nodded. She thought, maybe because his head moved, that he smiled. His questions continued.

"Do you often take so well to strangers?"

"You get used to them after a while. All of my family are frequently strangers; they show up among those you know and those you don't. You get used to it after a while. I always swore I'd never leave with a dark man who reminds me of my father, but here we are."

"Yes." Timothy leaned forward and this time she knew he was smiling. She saw, above his smile, the slight widow's peak she had traced the night before.

"Here we are," he said. She leaned back slightly and frowned.

"Well," he said, "we won't be here much longer. It shouldn't take them long to fix the pickup. Do you need more lemon for your tea?"

"I get tired, you know, of talking about my tea."

The shadow of the waitress fell on Diana's eggs. She looked up for a moment, confused, wondering whether it had been the waitress who had asked her about the tea. She hadn't meant to be rude.

"No thank you," she said, in case the waitress had asked.

"What happened," he asked, "after your sister left?"

"We went to Florida for two weeks, and when we returned to the dining room, we were assaulted by the smell of sweet oranges quietly rotting in the monkey-pod bowl. I stared at the wallpaper, but I couldn't see my sister among the vines, and we never saw her name in the headlines. In the late afternoons my mother dusted picture frames and put out sunflower seeds for the chickadees. My father sat silently, heavily in the armchair until it pressed dents into the floor. I began to wish it would press holes in the floor, collapse the floor, and carry him down to the wet boxes and cobwebs of the basement.

"In the evenings I listened to the violins, but they were interrupted by the piano. My father would stand, blocking the speakers and mumble about the grave deficiencies of the stock market. My mother would try to answer reasonably, but the iron's steam would get in her eyes. The weeks went on in this way. I can't remember for sure. At times I thought maybe years went on in this way. They do sometimes, you know."

Timothy nodded and handed her the salt.

"Some evenings I sat on my bed and stared at the window. There was nothing in the sky. Maybe a moon, but I didn't notice. I thought about meeting you and wondered whether, when you walked slowly across the room, I'd even notice you. I knew that my sister would have noticed. Jessica would have laughed. She laughed at night, frequently. Once I did, but a long time ago. You wouldn't remember, even my mother doesn't remember. She remembers when I screamed at night. In those days things came in the window—an old black woman, a staring man, coins on my sheet. In the morning my throat was always sore."

Diana put down the salt.

"Things behave more properly now. Cats drop from the trees, runners run in the street, stars remain on the outside of the window, and you sit patiently on the other side of the table, asking about my tea."

He smiled at her, head tilted, as if expecting her to smile back, but she looked down at her tea. When she tasted it, it was sweeter than before, and the shadow of the window frame moved away from the saltshaker and fell off the edge of the table. She could feel Timothy's gaze on her right shoulder. When she rested her hand there, she noticed the skin of her hand.

"Things will go easier when we can get moving again," he said. "For now, at least, we can get out of here; we can go on outside."

After he paid the bill, they sat on the curb in front of the diner and watched the mechanic knock different-sized wrenches against the orange pickup. At first Diana tried to pay attention to the stories Timothy told her; then she kicked off a sandal to feel the dirt pushed up against the edge of the curb. Flies crawled up her leg.

"This dirt resembles the dirt you described in your stories," she said. "The dirt that lay on the wildflowers and under the cafe signs, that accumulated in the folds and creases of your black leather jackets when you rode motorcycles through the mountain towns on weekends between Memorial Day and the Fourth of July. It makes me think of cinnamon."

"Doesn't taste like cinnamon."

"We used to keep large cans of cinnamon for the fall when we made apple crisp and applesauce. And each year we had to use twice as much cinnamon as the year before. If I knew you then, I'd have spread you like bread dough on the kitchen table, and sprinkled cinnamon and raisins all over."

She pushed her finger along the inside fold of his elbow, then rubbed the finger clean against the skin of her leg. Timothy began to talk again, and Diana shivered. The curb was now in the shade. He told her he couldn't understand how she could still be cold, and he led her to the picnic table in the sun.

"Sit here and warm up." He indicated the picnic bench. "Be sure and watch out for splinters." He stood behind her and they looked off to the east—toward Missouri or Tennessee.

"Listen," she said after a while. "Somewhere in the distance, or behind the garage, someone's imitating the sound of a motorcycle or a chain saw. Do you hear? They're starting and stalling and starting again. The sound bounces like the light, it rattles. It's a harsh light, and it goes on diluting color, revealing old toenails, flattening skunks, landing here on the grasshoppers and there on the dry grass; it's like the light, several summers ago, that struck the towels on the line. They were bright pink in the morning when we hung them out, but they grew pale by afternoon. That August, after a morning watching clothes dry on the line, we spent the afternoon in our neighbor's compost heap digging, lifting the wilted flowers from the warm ash, burying the birds and small mice the cat left on the porch and under the lawn chairs. We assumed they were dead. I don't know how to explain this to you, but once, by the trashcan, a dead gray mouse grew thinner in the afternoon sun. The light moved his whiskers like milkweed, and the fly crawling over him was half as big as his head. I watched him, and when the ants started to taste his nostrils, I worried about the night."

Timothy said she'd been drinking too much tea.

"I'll get you a beer," he said. "Stay here."

He stretched and walked to the restaurant's screen door. When he emerged with two bottles, he walked toward the garage. Leaning over the mechanic's shoulder he peered into the insides of the pick-up.

"What did you see?" Diana asked when Timothy returned.

"How could I possibly see anything," he answered with disgust. "It's dark in there."

He set down the bottles.

"My eyes can't possibly adjust, because of this. He swept his hand in front of him with the palm turned up. It was cupped to hold the light or to hold his disgust.

"Your hand is curved," Diana said. "It's permanently curved by the years spent gripping black motorcycle handles. If I straightened your fingers, they would creak like stairs at night."

He looked at her intently. The grass turned brown; fires started in the distance.

"I can't figure you out," he said, "or your sister either. Most of the time, you aren't all here, and when you're here, it's as if you're about to leave."

"How could I be bothered to leave at this point? What am I going to do—walk out there and stick out my thumb?" Imitating his gesture, she stretched her arm toward the horizon. With her upturned arm she indicated the distance, but her gesture stopped halfway as she watched a scab crawl toward her elbow. A minute crawled along as well, and then a second.

"While you were gone, while you were getting the beer, the motorcycle started again, still with too much treble, but this time it managed to keep its engine running and it moved, like an airplane, off to the west."

Her finger pointed toward the air above the horizon.

"If I concentrate," she said, "I can still focus on that gray speck of sound. I concentrate so I'm not startled by the men in the upper left corner of my left eye. I don't know why they are always blond, and," she drank from her beer, "I don't know where I kicked off my sandals."

She sat calmly, as if the pressure of Timothy's boot against her instep did not bother her, as if she were not thinking about her sandals. Her little finger made commas on the outside of the bottle.

"In the evenings," she said, "after our bath, Jessica and I drew pictures on the fogged-over windows. The pictures weren't much, but we enjoyed the squeak of fingers against the glass. Suddenly we'd be disgusted, and we'd smear over the panes with our whole hands. Our hands would be wet, and the glass would have uneven streaks of water. So we'd slap each other and then we'd get slapped. She could always hit harder than me."

"When you talk about Jessica," Timothy said, "I remember a girl I met on the other side of a room in Pueblo. She looks a little like you, but her hair is curly."

"I guess it was her you were looking for when you walked across the room and ran into me."

Timothy lay back on the picnic bench and watched her back.

"I wasn't looking for anyone; I was just walking across the room," he said. "But it sounds like the same person to me. You know, you'd better drink your beer before it goes flat."

Instead, Diana stared at the bubbles that rose infinitely from a spot halfway down the bottle. "I already told you my sister is dead," she thought, but she didn't remember whether she had told him. She tried the words anyway.

"I already told you my sister is dead."

Timothy may not have heard her. He sat up, shrugged, and said, "Sounds like the same person to me."

Diana stood, brushed off her shorts, and walked away from the garage and diner. She walked toward the road where she held out her arm, curving and straightening her thumb. After a while, when no cars came by and the skin on her underarm began to turn pink, she walked back to the picnic table and saw that Timothy was asleep. The motorcycle, after disappearing hours before, thickened on the horizon. Diana thought at first the sound was the red ant that had crawled into her ear as she finished her beer.

When Timothy woke, the pickup was ready. When they walked toward it, he said, "I bet you never thought we'd get out of here."

"I never thought," said Diana, and she climbed up into the passenger seat. It was a long way up. For the first seventeen miles, as they drove toward the sun, the truck's shadow fell on the freckles of Diana's right arm, and she refused to look at Timothy. She tried to focus on the horizon, but the motion of the plains carried her gaze back to the hood of the truck.

"Let me know when you want me to drive."

He nodded, but he did not seem to be listening. His right hand played with the radio knob. After several miles passed quietly and not quickly, he asked her about her sister.

"I don't see why you want to talk about her."

"What else can we do? When there's nothing but static on the radio, you might as well fill me in on the time your sister left."

"She left, she died, she died, she left." Diana shook her head and frowned. "I don't know how to tell that story. Maybe if I heard three notes of music, played in the right order, I could get the words right." She stared out the window for a while. "There isn't any music, so I can do no more than watch those markers go by."

A green mile marker approached the truck—476—and Diana counted carefully the thirteen stakes between it and the next mile marker—475. Timothy's hand stopped playing with the radio dial; instead, it smoothed the cotton front of his tee shirt. Eventually he reached for her cheek, and she withdrew to the corner by the window. The button pressing against her temple felt like her father's thumb.

Thirty miles farther west Timothy found a song on the radio. The bass, as usual, was slower than the treble. The sun, as usual, had a hard time pushing through the dirt on the window.

"There's music now," Timothy said. "Listen to the notes and you can find the words."

"In those years," she said, "our parents were voices in the kitchen at night. My mother's voice was hard and high, and it came from the space behind her back molars. In our bed, Jessica and I wouldn't speak, and after she was fourteen Jessica never cried or wet the sheets. When it was hot, in the summer, we'd stretch our toes to the dark corners, and when they met, our toes would tie in knots. I'll show you tomorrow."

She thought the song did not contain the right combination of notes; she thought it moved too quickly. Her words could not keep up.

"In the mornings we watched the rose vines turn on the wallpaper. Later there would be thumbprints between the blue roses. In the afternoons we drew with crayons on the wall, and in the early afternoons of the following months we stripped the leaves of the houseplants and piled them on the dining room table." She paused. "We've lost that station, so I can't tell you anymore. You might as well turn off the radio now."

Timothy continued to drive, and they continued toward the west. The flat light grew deep. Occasionally the plains turned green and neat and were boxed by white fences in the small towns. As they passed, left-handed women mowed the grass in the cemeteries. Gray cats limped after the truck. Later, the moon knocked against the front windows of the houses, leaving traces of blood.

After midnight they spent what was left of the night in a cornfield. They lay in the back of the pickup, and the ribs of the bed pressed against the ribs of Diana's back. She used Timothy's bony arm for a pillow and wondered when the rasp that followed every ninth breath would separate from Timothy's lips and settle in her throat; she wondered when the grasshoppers would begin to move.

When she began to talk, it had begun to grow light, but Timothy was not yet awake.

"I could tell you a lot if I thought you weren't listening," she whispered. "I could tell you that I've always been afraid of wide spaces, and although I might explore what I once feared, I'm not particularly fond of bony pillows on the high plains. I could tell you that I didn't kill my sister, though I longed to. I nearly killed my father, but that hardly counts: I told him why she was gone. I wouldn't tell you. He sits peacefully now in the blue armchair, with one leg on the footstool, and one foot near the floor. His mouth opens slowly, and when the robin moves across the window his blue eyes may move, but his head doesn't turn. My mother whistles in the kitchen and rearranges bowls of fruit.

"My sister buried two babies, then cut off her hands. They weren't her babies anyway. She was just fourteen and I carried her body to the orchard before midnight. In the early morning I spread leaves and apples over her and braided her hair with the orchard grass. In the evening white-faced hornets crawled among the apples."

Watching from his elbow, Timothy unzipped her sleeping bag and the warm sweat between her legs turned clammy beneath his hand.

"You get nightmares from the heat; you've got to be careful," he said. "In the summer, goose down can be dangerous." He licked his hand and replaced it. Then, one after the other, he bent her knees so that the toes emerged from orange nylon. Diana opened her mouth and felt Kansas on the back of her tongue.

Timothy said, "You're the first person I've met who has nightmares while they're awake."

"I could tell you of others."

"Tell me." He separated her knees, and when he held her limp right leg, the calf swung listlessly.

"When your body's curled around my knees," she said, "the hairs that grow from your back, toward my face, frighten me. And if I know that it's too dark to see the hairs on your back, I also know that it's too early to be accosted by a stranger in the back of a pickup. You lie here, chewing about my kneecap, pressing my skin and your bottom lip between your teeth, and Jessica lies in an old orchard among the rotten apples and the hornets' husks.

"Of course, they were my mother's babies. Not Jessica's, not even mine. More likely Jessica's than mine. She already knew strangers in the orchard. She called them soldiers—the tall soldier, the gray soldier, the one with the limp. She offered to share, but I pretended she was teasing. I preferred to watch from the shed. I stood there alongside the lawn mower, the soft caterpillars, the sticky cocoons in the window. I was not ready. Besides, her legs were longer than mine.

"My mother did not consider them babies, but I wouldn't call them embryos. They were large for that. When she carried them, she walked briskly; when we buried them, her back sagged, and she wore down the heel of her right shoe. We thought my father, when he came in from the garage, never noticed the difference."

When Timothy began to stroke her back, she considered allowing him to continue until afternoon, but she rolled away and collided with the side of the truck bed. He leaned back and extended his arms along the rim of the bed.

"Some of the things you say don't always make sense to me."

"I don't know why you'd expect them to make sense."

He looked past her to the fields, toward bright spears of corn just emerging from the cracked dirt. He buttoned his jeans.

"Something you said about your sister. Something about her hands."

"It's a story. I told you," said Diana. "You can't expect everything to make sense in a story." She rolled up the sleeping bag and wedged it into the spare tire.

As they drove, she watched the rows of corn fanning from her. No longer were there individual stalks, but inverted Vs, rows changing place with rows. Easily you could be mesmerized by changing rows of corn; easily enticed by slow back rubs.

Before the heat of midday Diana drove, and the steering wheel was higher than she expected. Timothy slept, slumped toward her on the seat, and while she marveled at his trust, Diana made sure his hair didn't touch her bare arm. When a speck thickened in the sky, she thought it was an airplane, although it might have been a grasshopper. The wipers caught grasshoppers and spread them on the windshield. She smelled the pebbles at the edge of the road and said, "The evening when Jessica came in from the orchard without any soldiers and without any hands, blue roses faded on the bedroom wall. We found her hands later, beside a stump; we didn't find any soldiers. After that we went to Florida, and when we came back my mother piled eggshells and orange peels in the corner of the library."

"We could go to Florida, if you like," Timothy said. "We could go there now." Diana was silent; then she said, "You're supposed to be asleep."

"Problem is, we're headed in the wrong direction."

Diana moved the pickup into the left-hand lane to pass a Volkswagen. She checked the rearview mirror and pulled back to the right. An exit was approaching.

Timothy said, "How could your sister cut off her own hands? Could she, by herself?"

Diana did not respond for a long while. Grasshoppers leapt before the truck. Of course she couldn't hear their cries. It could be that he was looking at her. She did not need to notice.

"My mother spent hours of every afternoon chasing gray squirrels from the bird feeder. I spent hours between my sheets. At night screams came in the window, and during the day the walls changed color—the white background of wallpaper turns cream-colored over time. In the morning, sunlight would land behind the bed and the hands would walk up the wall. The thumb catches up with the little finger; then the little finger escapes again. Before they begin, they're dipped in blood."

Diana reached for the vinyl dashboard. It had softened in the sun. Timothy glanced at her hand, then slumped down in his seat, closing his eyes.

As he slept, the airplane Diana was watching remained before her, although it banked, occasionally, to the right. When he woke it was late afternoon, and she said, "All the time you were sleeping, the stripes on the road came too quickly toward the truck, and each time you touched your ear I thought it was my father's. Then as your mouth changed its shape, the plane I was watching tuned into a hawk and landed on a fencepost behind the truck."

Timothy nodded. "You better let me drive now."

It would be easy, she thought, to ride beside him for many more days. They could ride and stare at the window glass, and let it be easy, just for a while.

They changed drivers, and near the mountains, the afternoon turned into evening and settled into the bed of the truck.

Diana cranked down the window, opening her mouth as the wind struck her face and neck. It dried her mouth and her white teeth; her tongue would not move. She wanted that wind to wash over all her limbs, her body, wanted the wind that scoured what pale paint was left on the faded pickup to scour her own pale skin.

She told Timothy to stop the truck. She told him she wanted to ride in the back.

"Just for a little while," she said.

"I don't know that that's safe."

"It's not a problem. We did it all the time when we were kids. We sat in the pickup bed next to the boxes of apples as the old pickup did its best to speed on down the highway. Sometimes you smelled the winey-sweet smell of apples, sometimes not."

In the back she shifted her weight and shifted it again, trying to get comfortable on the ribs of the bed. She did not feel right, where she sat behind the cab. The wind tossed the cab's shadow sideways left and sideways right, but did not brush hard against her skin. Halfway crouched, she crept to the side of the truck, the passenger's side, away from the rear window, away from the dark shape of Timothy's head. Maybe he could see her in the mirror, maybe not. Why would he bother to look?

She pictured herself grabbing the side of the bed, pulling herself up, still in a crouch like a crow, up onto the side of the pickup. The crow's feathers were split and pushed backwards by the wind. Between the parted feathers, white flesh showed. Purple and green glints leapt like elves from the deep and terrible plumage. She pulled herself up and wobbled on the bed's edge like a wobbling crow. Keeping her balance took all the focus and muscle she could manage in the battering wind. She watched herself uncurl her claws and with gleaming wings spread, catch the oncoming wind, glint for a moment in the sun before banking off to the right.

The Bridge

Sometimes I stand at the window for hours and watch the bridge cross the creek. Sometimes my mother calls while I watch the bridge; I have been receiving a lot of telephone calls lately. The bridge is old and has trouble stretching from this bank to the other side of the creek. It is sunburned from long days of exposure, and flakes of its paint fall into the water. On the bridge, pedestals stand where there ought to be statues.

People are coming this evening and there are too many things to do. All the same, my mother calls while I'm busy watching the bridge, and she explains about the dresses of growing children. "If you put tucks in their hems," she says, "then lengthening is no problem." My mother, I suppose, is concerned about bare knees. I flatten the piles of dust rising in the corners of the window sash and notice that no children are playing on the bridge.

"At the filling station," my mother says, "they ought to have special hoses to fill the tires of baby strollers."

Now I see some children on the bridge, but more will come out in the morning. They pose on the bridge and imitate statues. Tomorrow, maybe, statues will imitate the children.

My mother continues, "I changed the thermostat setting from 69 to 67, but there's no significant change in the length of pauses when the furnace is not on. Of course, there may be a difference in the wind chill factor at night. What do you think?"

I give the phone to Bart, and he coils the phone cord around his neck.

Sometimes Bart listens patiently to my mother on the phone. Sometimes he thinks he's in love with me. He has been patient with me for years and he says he would rather talk to my mother than to my friend Ada who thinks my mother is mad. She knows her mother is mad. She expects, probably, that all mothers are mad. "There are signs," she says and two drops of coffee fall from her coffee cup. She lists some signs: the dog collar dangling from the dining room light fixture, the back-up light of the Oldsmobile replaced with a green Christmas tree bulb, the Berol pencils inscribed with name, address, zip code, and telephone number. "But," Ada warns, "these signs may vary."

Bart says the signs don't mean anything, or at least they don't mean my mother is mad. He says a carved pencil is just a carved pencil, and the signs may be signs of character.

I've decided it's easy with signs to attribute them to character. It's easier not to worry about where character leaves off and madness begins.

Although I've received a lot of phone calls lately, Ada has not called. I wonder if she has met anyone in Arizona. She got pregnant on vacation in Cancun, and after her husband left her, she decided to have the baby in Arizona. She thought the consistency in temperature might be important for the baby. I want her to call because her last letter was enticing. I need her to call because, except for all the people dying, there's been little adventure in my own life lately: I'd like to know about some adventure. I can only get adventure from my friends' lives since television is make-believe, and they don't write books about adventure anymore; they only write books about words.

I begin to arrange ashtrays for the evening. After a while the telephone rings. I've been receiving a lot of telephone calls lately. The phone call isn't about the ad I haven't placed in the paper. It's my mother. She says she forgot to tell me about the red pickup that ran over my cousin's tricycle three weeks ago last Tuesday. I begin to think Ada is right. I stand listening to the receiver and Bart stands close to me, without touching. I can't feel the hairs of his flannel shirt on my cheek, but I notice the air they stir. He wants me to stop listening to my mother and pay attention to him; he wants me to fill the ice trays for this evening.

While Bart frequently derides Ada, he doesn't suspect that she disapproves of him. Like most of my friends, Ada encourages me when I meet a new man. Like most of my friends, when she meets the man, she does not approve. She says Bart is more interested in his bicycle than in me. She may be right. She hasn't written or called recently, but, at least, I imagine she will write soon: she wouldn't want to be alone when the baby is born.

While we place ice trays on the porch railings to freeze, Bart tells stories to entertain me. His stories have little adventure; they concern phenomena that interest him. Bart is not quite the hero I had in mind, but he is patient with me. Neither, I suspect, is he quite the hero he had in mind, and to entertain me he tells me about the mud puddles he explored during his leisure hours last summer.

In the evening Bart's friend Enoch arrives, and later that evening more of Bart's friends arrive carrying a small child and a large bottle of Highland Mist. I cut slices of banana bread to go with the scrambled eggs, and later Bart's friends play with the knives. When the telephone rings for the third time, I wait for the message to come on. As I listen to my mother's voice, I learn about a woman in the Bahamas who was caught in the propeller blades of her boat. The message resembles a postcard. "You should have been there," it says. I look at the black window and cannot imagine that there were ever any children on the bridge. After eleven I stop worrying that my mother will call again, and I wonder how fast I will have to drink to catch up with the others. I look into the living room—Bart's friends are slashing stems of the baby spiders as they dangle from the spider plants. I come into the room with a large glass of whiskey and sit on the couch.

Bart pretends to be listening to his friends as he refills their beers. He speaks to Elena, smiling, and glances at the cat in the window. I pretend that he looks at me and smiles when I look away. I keep on looking away and I think about the phone call. I don't know what to do with the woman caught in the propeller blades. I don't know what to do with her arms. Who will untangle them? My fingers won't move; my ideas don't agree.

The other people in the room don't always agree tonight.

"We have to decide about going to Richard's grandmother's funeral," Alphonse says. "How many cars?"

"Who's going to sit in the back?" Mira asks. "I'm tired of sitting in the back." She drops a slice of lemon into her cup and the tea changes color.

I can't tell if it is the night that's unsettled, or if I'm unsettled. After a while it's obvious that there's no difference. This is one of those times when everyone I know is dying, or when everyone I know knows someone who has died. It's at these times that my friends have miscarriages, that my mother calls and tells me about the propeller blades on sightseeing boats, that Bart's friends persuade us to attend miscellaneous funerals.

I watch Bart's friends talk, and I watch them suck the ice cubes from their drinks. I realize they want to talk to me, but I don't have time to listen. Bart sits back in his chair, smiling. He isn't smiling at me. The cat's white bib shows in the window. The cat isn't smiling at me either. I decide to go out. When I walk down the stairs toward the street I begin to walk more slowly. Soon there will come a time when the foot that's behind will have great difficulty passing the foot that's not behind.

On Saturday we argue about the funeral, and Bart inserts bits of bacon into the yolk of his fried egg when my mother calls. She asks if the water in the creek was rising, was close to the bridge. She wonders because she heard on the news that there was flooding in Missouri.

"I don't live in Missouri," I say.

"Yes. I know, but you know all of those rivers are related; sometimes they resemble each other. Speaking of rivers, have you heard from your friend Ada lately? Did she get back from the Caribbean?"

"Ada didn't go to the Caribbean. She went to Mexico, and now she is in Arizona, waiting for her baby to be born. I should be hearing from her any time."

My egg yolk is congealing, growing dark, and I suspect that the children are falling off the bridge. My mother asks when I will go stay with Ada.

"I haven't decided about that yet."

Bart's fork scrapes his plate. When I hang up the phone, he says we should leave for the funeral at eleven.

"You know I can't go," I say. "My face is growing pale."

"It's all right for you to make excuses," he says, "but you always expect me to do the right thing. Besides, the funeral might not be so bad. Everyone will be there. Milt and Sandra are driving up from Oklahoma in their '63 Mustang. It's been a long time since I've seen that car. Anyway, I won't go without you."

"Fine," I reply, but at 10:45 he drags me by the cuff of my sweater into the car and drives with one hand on the steering wheel and the other on the clasp of my seatbelt, to hold it closed, to keep me from escaping. I'm enjoying myself; I spend the drive to the church imagining how he will get me out of the car and into the pew.

At the cemetery after the funeral, everyone there is wishing it would rain so they can run for the cars. I want to run for the cars. I don't want to think of the fifteen lawyers who, my mother said, gathered at the back of the sightseeing boat and stared over the edge at the woman who jumped too soon. I glance at the cars, and a moment later I glance again. If I take one step back and two steps sideways . . . Bart's glove tightens on my elbow. "You can wait a bit longer," he whispers. "It's only decent."

He's the only one whispering, and I'm not the only one measuring the distance between the grave and the cars.

I know that was a real woman in the Bahamas. The sharks knew she was real by the blood. The sunbathers on the front of the boat knew that she was no longer a real woman when the water turned red. I wonder, how red can green water become?

If the ground wasn't frozen, I know my feet would sink and seek the other bones that are heaped here and there, close by. I know others are thinking the same thing because they keep lifting their feet, like horses, and setting them down again. Bart is not lifting his feet. He's holding them firm and watching the tall girl in the long coat. I'm not sure I want to distract him. I'm not sure I could distract him, even if I did want to, but I focus on the question of desire. I look around at everyone standing about, at everyone except the girl in the long coat. All the people standing about are thinking the same things differently—thinking about how they are not sad that Richard's grandmother finally died, thinking about how they would like to sit, even if it's only in the back seat. And while we are standing there it does not begin to rain. It is too cold to rain.

A few months later, on a Monday, my mother arrives for an extended visit. It's two days before she notices that Bart isn't here.

"Whatever happened to Bart?" she asks.

"Nothing happened to him. You know he has to travel a lot on his business."

"What *is* his business?"

"It involves travelling a lot."

I don't decide not to tell her that Bart left to look for Ada in the desert. I just don't tell her. Bart left because he was bored. He left to look for adventure in the desert. I hope he finds it. I know he found Ada. I haven't been receiving a lot of phone calls lately, but I've received a lot of postcards. They send me postcards once a week. Once every two weeks.

The postcard with the giant cactus says: Sunny weather. Not a lot of puddles. Not a lot of people. A lot of cactus and dried bodies in the desert.

The postcard of the red sunset says: We leave for vacation in a month—after the baby is born. We think of going to the Bahamas. Wish you were here.

The postcard with the tombstone says: It's a boy. Naming him after you. Love, Bart and Ada.

I stare out the window at the bridge while my mother puts the groceries away and tells me about the brown paper bags. While I consider the empty pedestals on the bridge, a small boy climbs onto one of them. He waves his arms like a hawk. I don't know why he should have trouble keeping his balance since the pedestal is quite wide.

My mother says, "You don't really need to leave your paper bags in such a mess. The best way to store paper bags is to fold all the ones that are the same size and put them into an open bag of the same size."

I pretend I'm listening. Instead, I'm thinking about the bridge. I think it's convenient for this bridge to be in a place where water can run under it and keep it cool in the summer. There are bridges in less convenient places, like the desert. I wonder what those bridges do all day, just sitting on the sand. That's where they took London Bridge. They can take this bridge there, too, for all I care. Maybe Bart misses it, but I doubt it.

My mother bangs the cupboard in the kitchen. She's still talking about the bags. To placate her I ask, "What about the plastic ones?" I hope she didn't tell me about the plastic bags while I was thinking of the bridge, or I hope she doesn't remember that she told me.

"Plastic bags," she says, "are a whole other ballgame. Those opaque ones they use for freezer bags, they aren't nearly as strong. And what have you heard from your friend Ada? Her baby must be due by now. I think a little girl would be nice, don't you? Or is she one of those people who knows what the baby is before it's born? I don't understand that at all. You'd think they could be patient for nine months."

I hope that she'll continue to talk if I fold the paper bags obediently. She only expects answers occasionally, and I can usually manage to pick and choose the questions I answer. But she's looking at me now, and I realize she is not talking.

"You do keep in touch with Ada," she says.

"Yes, of course. I had a postcard the other day. It had a sunset on it. You know the desert is famous for its sunsets. She had a little boy—seven pounds, two ounces. In a couple of weeks, she's going to go on vacation in the Bahamas. She says she needs a rest."

"Seven pounds. That's a nice size. You be sure and tell her to be careful when she goes snorkeling. We don't want to leave that poor baby an orphan. No mother. No father."

I help my mother put away the groceries. I don't tell her about the father. My mother tells me about the can of shrimp bisque she found at the back of the supermarket shelf. "Do you know," she says, "its price is marked seven cents lower than the can on the front of the shelf." She leaves the can in the middle of the sink so that I'll notice it later.

"Do you know," she says, "when we get the groceries put away, I think I'll go out and take a little walk before we eat."

I'm relieved that she doesn't ask me to go with her. I couldn't go anyway. I have to fix supper. While she is gone, I take a hot bath in the empty apartment. I'm glad to be alone. And for the first time, I'm even glad that Bart isn't here to disturb the silence. After I finish my bath, I fix supper: I open the can of shrimp bisque and pour it into the sauce pan. While I'm putting the can opener away the phone rings and that surprises me. I haven't been receiving a lot of phone calls lately. It's Bart. So much for the empty apartment.

For a while he talks about diapers and plane reservations. He asks about my mother. I say she is fine, that she went for a walk, but that she should be back soon. I stretch the cord so that I can see the bridge out the window. It isn't dark yet.

"What I really wanted to tell you," Bart says, "was that you were right about all mothers being mad."

"It wasn't me who said that. It was Ada. She used to tell me that my mother was mad. She used to think that all mothers are mad."

"Well, now she's a mother. She can join the crowd."

I'm looking at the people on the bridge as they look at the window expecting to see themselves, but the angle is wrong.

Bart says, "Ada is obsessed with diapers and talcum powder. She will only talk in whispers. She is worried about thrush. I thought only horses got thrush. Do you think Ada thinks she has given birth to a little horse? She's completely mad. She leaves the light on all night in the bathroom and cries more often than the kid. It's not a bad kid, but it doesn't look at all like a horse."

I am comparing the costumes of the people on the bridge. Portions of the hems are down on the skirts of all the women who are wearing skirts. I see my mother come slowly back over the bridge. She pulls herself up next to the child who is waving his arms on the pedestal, pretending he is a hawk, or pretending he is about to fall.

Bart says, "I can't imagine how we're going to manage the plane ride to the Bahamas."

"Oh, yes," I respond. "My mother says Ada should be careful when she jumps off of sightseeing boats."

"I can't even imagine that we'll get as far as a boat. Ada will be too busy sprinkling talcum powder in the toilet and taping pampers to the window. Why did you gasp?"

"My mother just jumped off the bridge. I saw her come back from her walk while you were talking about the different types of baby formulas. Then she just climbed up on the edge of the bridge and jumped off."

"Oh," Bart responds and asks about his purple toothbrush; he wants to take it to the Bahamas. I tell him I can't keep track of his toothbrushes.

"You can't keep track of a lot of things," he says. "Listen, I've got to hang up—the baby's crying."

"Right," I say. "Be careful in the Bahamas."

Stray Socks

Late one Sunday in April, Clara woke up in the baby's room. She felt ill, she felt sleepy, and she had difficulty remembering her dream. The baby wasn't in the room with her; the baby was singing in the living room. Clara did recall that last winter she had watched an old sweatshirt fade on the clothesline. There had been many disasters in the winter. She didn't recall what caused the disasters, but she knew that before spring she was tired of being so serious, and that she'd considered running away with the sixteen-year-old neighbor boy. She didn't actually consider that. It was something she pretended to help her get through the hard days. When she was a child, she'd frequently pretend things to get through the hard days—pretend she was in a story: she'd ride in a covered wagon along the Oregon Trail; she'd lean out of a helicopter window during a flood, helping the people climb off their rooftops; she'd pretend she was a mom, living in a yellow house with, maybe, half a dozen children. Soon Clara would get out of the warm cot to check on the children who were not at all pretend, of whom there were not, thank goodness, half a dozen. Three was quite enough—the two boys and baby Dolores. She could hear the television since her husband was, of course, watching the game, and she could hear someone laughing. That was Jack, of course. Jack was seven and he was quick to find any situation hilarious. "It's not funny," Amos would say. Amos was a year older. "How can you think everything's so funny?"

Clara thought other children would show up occasionally—on television commercials, on the bus that went by and didn't stop at the bus stop in town. She decided that lost children must return as nuthatches return to the feeder when it is finally filled after two empty weeks.

Lee came into the room between innings of the game. "Are you just going to lie here all day? Are you sick? Are you hungry?"

"I'm not hungry. I'm just tired. I've just been lying here, wondering what it would be like if we'd never happened to run into each other."

"Well, for one thing, there'd be three less children in this town."

"Fewer."

"You always have to be the one who is right."

"I'll get up pretty soon. It's pretty silly, lying here in bed when the sun is out."

"Laying."

She made a face. There was no point responding. He didn't care if it was laying or lying, but he did know the difference.

He sat on the edge of the bed instead of on the chair. She stiffened, but she didn't move over to make room. She told him that earlier that afternoon she'd had a dream, and something awful had occurred. It was after she woke up that she wondered whether she'd been in the dream.

"Not much of a dream, if you can't remember what it was about or whether you were in it."

"Some dreams are like that."

She wished he would get off the bed, but she wouldn't tell him so. She just lay there, wishing.

He asked if their sixteen-year-old neighbor boy was in her dream.

"As far as I remember, no one was in the dream. Maybe it happened in the other room. I don't remember, exactly. The longer I lie here, the farther away the dream is."

He got up and told her he had to get back to the game. "You could come see how the kids are doing, or you could sleep a little more."

"I'll be in a minute or two," she said, but very soon after he left, she fell asleep again.

She slept until the light changed. When she woke, she was nearly certain that maybe the room had changed. After all, when she woke from her naps that spring, sometimes she was sleeping on the cot next to the baby's crib and sometimes she was on her own bed, sleeping on the bedspread with the baby asleep beside her. Once in a while there were notes under the pillow that confused her, and at times when she heard shooting in the hall, she tried to count the guns. Today there was no note under the pillow, and although she didn't know where Ralph was, she was almost certain he was not in the house and was not playing with the children in the living room. Ralph had rarely come around when Lee was home. Ralph was the sixteen-year-old who had lived next door. She'd met him at the clothesline the winter before this April afternoon, the afternoon she told Lee about her strange dream. The clothesline was tied to a tree, and Ralph, leaning against the tree, had hair that was nearly the same color as the tree bark. He'd asked her if the blue jeans would dry before they froze.

"Not much chance of that," she'd said.

He'd looked confused, but then he smiled as if he understood. He understood, most likely, the two meanings possible in her words. Maybe he'd determine the appropriate meaning from future context. Clara left the clothesbasket under the clothesline and walked to the wood pile where she placed logs in the wood carrier.

"I'll carry that, if you like," he said.

"Thanks. I can manage." She nodded at him. Better than you, she thought; he was very thin. "Come in for some tea, if you like."

That Sunday afternoon in April Clara decided she ought to get out of bed soon—as soon as she remembered her dream. It was beginning to come to her. It was about a rape. Hers. Someone, not Ralph, was in the dream. Not much chance that Ralph could have raped her. He was too thin, and she was too strong. Clara kept trying to remember the funny thing about the rape. Maybe the funny thing was that she couldn't remember it clearly. It wasn't a memory; it was an uneasy feeling that moved in her chest after she woke, or after she turned away from the mirror. But she should get up now and find out whether the children shooting each other in the hall were using their fingers to shoot or using toy guns. As far as she knew, her boys had no guns, real or toy. They did have fingers. She lay there thinking she could go back to sleep. Or they could go to sleep. Jack could curl up on the landing and Amos, since it was early spring, could stretch out by the creek in the path of the gray men who wandered there. She should try to keep her springs separate from the winters, although, sometimes, that's difficult to do. It was spring now, by the calendar, and high time she stopped taking long naps in the late afternoon. It was last winter when Ralph, the boy next door, had come in with her for a cup of tea, his first cup with her. He was the son of an aging dance team, and a wide belt held up his blue jeans. After the second cup of tea, he'd lit up a joint. She took a long drag when he passed it to her, but only held the smoke in her mouth. Even so, his action worried her.

"You don't know me well enough yet to smoke in front of me," she said finally.

Ralph smiled at her with amazement and some delight. "Of course I know you well enough. Why did you say that?"

She thought he should be more shy, and that she heard the baby sing. She considered ways to deal with the marijuana smell before the boys came home from school or Lee returned from work. She could pull open the door of the stove and let wood smoke into the room. She could make spaghetti sauce and spill oregano on the burner. She could tell Lee that the boy next door followed her home and lit up a joint. The possibility of telling him what had happened always occurred to her last, if at all; it was usually the most uninteresting option. Maybe not this time.

She had put the kettle on the burner again. Before it boiled, Lee called and hinted at what he would do when he got home from work. She didn't respond. Not much later the dog discovered he was lying in the shade, and he moved to find a sunny spot on the deck. Then the tea was finished, and Clara brought in all the laundry with Lee's frozen blue jeans and shirt. She stood the bodiless jeans before the fire and the heat forced them to bend with pain. She spread the rest of the laundry on the backs of chairs and on the banister where a note from Lee was taped. From the hearth rug, baby Dolores sucked her toast and waved at the undershirts and white socks. Clara pulled the note from the banister but did not read it immediately.

Lee left notes in odd places. Clara found them when she was looking for a blue napkin among the placemats, when she was returning unused Kleenex to the box. She thought at first that she found them after they were recently written. Later, she decided she found them after they were recently secreted. Some notes had obviously been written months or years ago. One said, "I wanted our first child to be a girl. You knew that. Now, it seems that you produce boys just to spite me." She had found that note among Dolores's diapers. It had been written in pencil on green lines on green paper torn from a notebook. The note had been written, apparently, after Jack's birth.

When Ralph left, Clara didn't cover up the smoke in the house with smoke from the stove, and by the time Lee came home she had forgotten about the boy next door since she was irritated with Amos and Jack, crossing the living room on their hands, knocking the nearly dry socks into the soup, and she was disturbed by the dog, crying on the deck.

When Clara climbed out from between the warm sheets, there was no longer any noise in the hall or on the stairs. Either Lee had taken the children to play along the creek, or there were no children. She may have dreamed that part. She could get up and look for evidence, for blond hairs on the dark blue sweater or a shoelace in the bathtub; instead, she looked at the window blinds, then got out of bed to adjust them. She thought she drew fine lines, careful distinctions, between what had happened, and what might have happened—what she pretended or remembered. Sometimes she was mistaken in her thinking. She thought of Lee and the children by the creek. Did they speak to the unshaven men who peered out from the bushes? Did Amos wish he lived beside the creek? Did he wonder how long it took a man's skin to assume the same color as his clothes? She thought of Lee hanging out clothes on the line and a sixteen-year-old neighbor girl following him home, lighting a joint. The girl would be sitting barefoot on the counter when Clara got home from work. They'd be playing poker with kitchen matches and glassy eyes, and Clara, immediately, would be bored.

The second time Clara saw Ralph he was returning the magazine on Florida's resorts, and he had a bruise under his right eye. It wasn't, exactly, a black eye. Clara wasn't surprised by the bruise—that week Jack also had a bruise. The bruise was on his shoulder, and the colors were interesting. The bruise reminded her of dandelions and cherry tomatoes. Dishcloths and table grapes.

The old dog was sleeping on a rug by the fire, and Ralph knelt to scratch his ears. When Clara asked Ralph about his bruised eye, Jack and Amos burst from the closet.

"They always find a way," Ralph said.

She saw Ralph frequently that winter; she saw the children, with or without bruises, even more often. The laundry she hung on the clothesline froze in shapes that were increasingly strange. Lee scattered about odd notes and an occasional sock. Once he intercepted, impatiently, a phone call from next door. Clara ignored the socks and read the notes. One note, left under a pillowcase in the linen closet, said, "Did you gather up, in our living room, the broken pencils abandoned by green-eyed mountain climbers? Did you imagine menace in my most recent approach?" You ask too many questions, she thought, folding the note into a paper airplane, sailing it over the balcony of the loft.

Since it was still quiet in the hall, Clara got out of bed to look for the children. The boys were with Lee, next to the television set whose volume was turned down. Lee was watching the news, and the baby was on the floor beside the rocking chair, ripping out the pages of a magazine. Lee described a double play that had occurred during the baseball game he'd watched earlier. Then Amos complained that Jack was pushing him into the corner of the couch, and Lee asked Clara if she was feeling better. "Maybe a little," she responded. "It's just that I'm so tired." After dinner Clara dried the forks and placed them in the drawer where, two days earlier, there had been a note. The boys at the piano played the same song over and over. Not Chopsticks. Clara smiled. Her mother had always disapproved of Chopsticks. In those days, when she was a child, Clara never thought to wonder why. The note in the drawer had said, "Your daughter resembles you; note especially her cheekbones. But it's not likely, when she's older, that she'll show interest in an Irish tenor or a thin mountain climber."

As the boys waltzed a waltz, humming their song, Clara wished she could clear her mind of dreams she didn't remember and of the notes Lee had left around during the late winter and early spring, notes that now mentioned the boy next door nearly as often as they mentioned the children. Lee changed the channel on the television. Waltzing, the children straightened and rumpled the rug.

A little later Clara filled the bathtub, and after she'd turned off the water, the faucet continued to drip. When Amos refused to take a bath, she used an old bandana to clear an area in the fogged-over bathroom window. It was not yet dark outside. As they watched slow blue shadows reach toward the creek, snow fell from a tree and turned into a nuthatch. She left the water in the tub for the younger children, and while Amos put clean pajamas on his dirty skin, she washed Dolores with the little clown washcloth. After Dolores splashed the water and tried to drown her plastic duck, the soap grew so thin that Clara was forced to open a fresh bar. Inside the wrapper was a note with her name on it. She'd unfolded the paper. It was blank.

Clara spent the night as she'd spent the afternoon, on the cot in the baby's room. She was not sure she'd ever again sleep in a bedroom with Lee. She'd been sleeping with Dolores for a month, for more than a month, ever since the afternoon in early March when Lee arrived home from work earlier than usual. He came in, carrying groceries, as Ralph was just leaving, and he didn't bother to speak to her during the evening or at dinner. She felt icy, even before he turned her over in the bed that night. He was hardly the man she married, hardly the man she'd fallen in love with. No one could love, could be in love with that man, the one who knelt on the side of the bed, loomed over her.

Because she'd napped in the afternoon, Clara lay awake while the baby slept. She found the baby's moans and gurgles comforting, and she wondered for how many weeks and months Dolores would continue to gurgle, and how many years or months would pass before Jack and Amos would join the gray men who appeared quietly amongst the trees along the creek. On warm afternoons beside the creek, Jack would toss a baseball into the air while a grizzled man recalled trips on his motorcycle through northern Arizona. Sometimes Jack would catch the ball in his baseball mitt. Sometimes, he'd miss the ball, and it would roll into the long grass beside the path. Some evenings, Amos would emerge from the bushes and wander slowly along the edge of the road.

A few evenings later, that April, Lee came in at six, removed his coat, and told her that the house next door had been sold. There was snow on his mustache.

"I never noticed that you had a mustache," she said.

"I never knew you could have the baby ready for bed by six," he answered, dropping his coat on the chair by the door. He set his hat on the chair's arm. The arm of the chair was a lion's head, carved in wood. It growled at the unnecessary warmth.

"I'm so tired of this snow," Lee complained. "Don't the gods know it's supposed to be spring?"

"Supper's almost ready. I fed Dolores earlier. If you could just set the table."

Clara went into the bathroom because her stomach was cramping. She kept expecting her period to start, but there was only faint spotting on her underwear. No blood. The next day she took Dolores to the drug store with her, and she bought three pregnancy tests. She knew she'd never believe just one. While the baby was taking her nap, she performed the tests, one after the other, and they all had the same result: plus, plus, plus. She was crying when she called her mother, "I just don't know what to do." She said she'd been going to leave Lee anyway. "I was sure I would, but here I am, still, and anyway, Lee would never let me have the children on my own. And now this. And Dolores is barely one and a half. She's just a baby. And now this. And I can't have an abortion. I can't imagine such a thing."

Her mother said she hadn't realized things were so bad. She said having an abortion is something no one can imagine, at first. She said Clara and the children could come stay with her, of course.

Clara smiled. "You're so kind," she said, "but you know how much you like living alone. When you visit us, you're so relieved when it's time to go home. And we'd be much too crowded, stepping on each other's toes." She'd have to get a place, Clara said, only she didn't have much money, and Lee would never . . .

"And, besides," she said, "besides that—Oh god, the baby's awake. I have to go. I'll call you later."

On that Tuesday, and on most other days of April, Clara acted as she had during other Aprils. She made sandwiches for the boys' lunches and fed Dolores in the kitchen. She made sure the children's faces were clean and dropped dirty clothes in the washing machine. She hung out the laundry, planted the garden, and slept for a while in the afternoon. Some evenings when she folded the clothes there were fewer socks than she'd hung on the clothesline—she suspected low-flying hawks. At the end of the month there were fewer teeth. Jack lost a bottom tooth, and Amos ran into a baseball bat. When Clara stood at the clothesline, she stared at the house next door. It was empty now—whoever had bought it had not moved in. She imagined that Ralph had gone to live with the gray men who wandered along the creek bed. She thought that he gathered smooth pebbles and stacked them into short mountains. More often now, as she vacuumed the rug, or as she woke from her naps, she remembered the things that Lee wanted her to forget. She remembered the water dripping in the tub. She remembered when the rape wasn't a dream. She remembered a bruise on her own cheek. Now the first hummingbirds of the year attacked the feeder and each other, but that night in early March there had been no birds outside the window when she escaped from the rumpled bed. There had only been night on the bathroom window, and when she turned on the light, when her reflection finally appeared, it did its best to forget what had happened moments before.

Clara went into the living room when she'd finished washing the dinner dishes. She walked past Lee, sat on the couch, and tried to count the hummingbirds at the feeder. Counting was impossible because of their rapidly changing choreography. Three or four birds sucked from the small openings at the base of the feeder; two or three, at various times, stole places from the feeding birds, or hovered behind. She said to Lee, who was reading the paper in his armchair, "We've got to talk, now. I'm not going to go on like this."

Lee looked up, frowning. "I don't know what you're talking about."

She said she refused to live any longer with someone who abused her. And she wasn't going to wait until something happened to one of the children.

"I've never hurt the children." Lee's voice was loud.

"Not yet." Clara looked at the hummingbirds, then back at Lee. "I thought I'd leave with the children, but there's so little room at Mom's, and Angela has her own family, filling up her house. There's the homeless shelter, Women's Assistance. How horrible that would be for the children. It's simpler than that—for now, you'll have to move out. The house is as much mine as yours: you pay the mortgage, but my father paid the down payment for me, for us. And it will be easier for you to find a place—there's just one of you."

"You're crazy," he shouted.

Amos's frightened face appeared at the door. Then it disappeared.

"On top of everything else, there's the new baby. You must know I'm pregnant."

Lee stared at her. "How?" So he didn't know. His ignorance surprised her, pleased her—she didn't know why. She glanced at the hummingbird feeder, but the tiny birds had given up for the night. It was nearly dark.

She said he must remember the night he attacked her, the night he raped her. He must remember that, afterwards, she'd left the bed and gone to sleep in the baby's room. He responded that she'd had other company, during the winter. She looked at him scornfully.

"Does pretending I was involved with Ralph help you feel less guilty?"

"I hardly feel guilty."

"And that's how I know it's over, for us."

She said she'd go back to work at the library, a few months after the baby was born. Probably, her mother would help with the childcare. She did not say that he would pay family assistance for the children. He didn't have to hear that tonight.

"Do you expect me to leave tonight?"

"Tonight, you can stay in the bedroom, but tomorrow . . ."

"I'm going for a walk." He put on his jacket, then slammed the door behind him.

It could have been worse, she thought. It might get worse, she thought, and she felt awful. She got up from the couch and wondered what had happened to Amos. She felt certain as she was sick in the bathroom that Amos was gone, but she found him curled with the dog, asleep in the middle of her bed.

About Author

Tory Tuttle lives with her family and their animals in the mountains west of Boulder, Colorado

Printed in the USA
CPSIA information can be obtained
at www.ICGtesting.com
LVHW042101200624
783493LV00004B/477

9 781958 015025